THE LAND OF NOD

By

ROBERT M WHITBEY

ISBN: 978-0-578-78886-9

PROLOGUE

Three Weeks Ago

The old, crowded bus bounced along the pitted street. Several of the larger jolts made Willy clutch his backpack tightly. He unzipped the bag every so often to ensure the lid was still secured on the small metal canister cocooned in yellow tape. He knew there was no way it could come open accidentally, but he continued checking it anyway.

The bus stopped at Willy's apartment building just outside downtown Topeka. It was seven blocks away. Avory College, where he was a senior. He exited the bus along with several other young people and headed for the entrance to his building.

It was a warm day, and that usually meant Willy walked home. But it wasn't a normal day. Today was the day Willy would complete his senior project and ensure his admittance into the graduate school of his choice. Despite his anxiousness from carrying the canister, he was almost giddy as he entered the apartment building.

Three floors up, he got off and walked the short distance to his door. He fumbled to get his keys out of his pocket, causing his backpack to slip off his shoulder. It fell toward the thin carpet, and Willy spun his right hand to grab it. He missed the strap but caught the loop on top. After a deep breath, he stuck the key in the lock and opened the door.

His roommate, Terry, was inside and quickly rose from the couch. "Did you find it?" he asked excitedly.

Willy smiled widely. "Yep. It was right in the back of the freezer, where dad told he saw it when he was a student." He reached inside his backpack and pulled the yellow-taped canister out.

"And it's safe?" Terry asked, not venturing any closer.

"Absolutely," Willy stated with confidence. "Even outside the vessel, you'd have to lick the petri dish to get infected."

"I know, I just........," Terry stammered uneasily. "It's dangerous, you know?"

"Psshh," Willy replied. "By tomorrow, this will be the healthiest thing ever to exist on the planet."

Willy walked to the closest door and went inside followed closely by Terry. The room, which used to be Terry's bedroom, was shrouded in plastic sheeting. It covered the walls, the ceiling, and the floor. Two long plastic folding tables were setup up along one wall with many stacked plastic petri dishes and plastic boxes along with a variety of lab equipment and even a small refrigerator.

Near the only window, they had constructed a makeshift fume hood out of Plexiglas and duct tape. Instead of running the air outside, the outlet pipe ran through a series of filter boxes and emptied into the room. Other than two wooden chairs, there was no other furniture. Terry's bed was now relegated to the living room.

Willy took a seat at the fume hood and placed the canister inside. He put on some blue nitrile gloves and removed the yellow tape carefully inside the clear hood.

"Outline it again for me," Terry requested.

"Terry, man, we've been over this a hundred times," Willy said harshly without stopping his work.

"Humor me. We could get in a lot of trouble and I want to have my story straight before I get sent back to Pakistan."

"Well, it was your idea," Willy replied with a smile, still working the tape.

"I just asked you what would happen if Rabies was airborne. I didn't expect you to actually try and do it."

"It was a challenge, and I love a challenge. And when I realized it could be used to cure genetic diseases, I figured it would be a heckuva Senior project. We're gonna' change everything!"

"If we don't die or get thrown in federal prison first."

"Nah, we're not doing anything illegal, really."

"In the past week, we have stolen Rabies-infected tissue from your father's company and Ebola cultures from the college that they didn't even know they had. I think we'll be in some trouble, Willy."

"When I show Professor Sloan what I, what WE have created, he's going to crap his pants. Then he's going to geek out. No one has ever done this."

"And your father will protect us from prosecution, right?" Terry asked knowing the answer.

"Wealth has its privileges," Willy agreed. "Oh, man, Dad's going to geek out even more than Sloan. His company has never even dreamed of designing anything like what I, what we're making."

"We were lucky you were able to 'borrow' so much equipment from his company," Terry suggested, with emphasis on the word 'borrow.' "This CRISPR setup is state of the art." Terry took a seat at the table holding the equipment.

"I remember doing my first gene splicing when I was ten," Willy mused. "The CRISPR technology was rudimentary back then. You can get similar stuff on eBay now. What we're working with here….," he trailed off, shaking his head. "Luckily, dads got enough in his stockrooms that he won't miss any of it for a while. By then, we'll be done with it."

Terry smiled and got a faraway look in his eyes. "The most virulent genes from Ebola and Rabies lysed into a flu virus. It would be a devastating superbug."

"But were using it to vector replacement genes into DNA. We'll be able to cure Down's Syndrome, Spina Bifoda, Parkinson's, you name it." Willy finally got all the tape off of the aluminum canister. "Now, glove up so we can get to work."

***

Three days later, both young men stared down at the dead mouse in the tiny cage under the fume hood. Though it still twitched occasionally, they knew it was dead from the copious amounts of blood that had erupted from both ends of the animal over the last five minutes.

"That's all six mice," Terry observed. "All died within eight hours of injection. All six had only a mild fever right up to the bloody stool and vomit episodes five minutes before death." He took his gloves off and tossed them into the metal trash can. "I'll put him in the freezer with the others in a minute."

Willy stood up, still staring at the mouse. "I can't believe we did it," he breathed out. "We're geniuses." He looked at Terry. "Friggin' geniuses!"

"This is the beginning of an incredible journey, my friend," Terry stated.

"Absolutely!" Willy gushed. "We'll be able to insert any gene we want into a genome. Like I said, this will change everything!" Willy sat back down and got a serious look on his face. "Look, Terry, I've been thinkin'. Maybe we've been thinking too small. Maybe we should take this discovery to industry first. It'll be worth billions to whomever holds the patents. We could sell it outright, then do whatever we want for the rest of our lives. Retire in our twenties if we want to!"

"Maybe we should offer it to your father first?" Terry replied, almost absent-mindedly. He was digging into a small duffel bag Willy hadn't noticed before.

"Yeah, maybe," he said with mild bewilderment. "Why do you have a bag in here? It's a clean room."

Terry pulled a small revolver out and pointed it at Willy. "I've been doing some thinking, too."

Willy slowly raised his hands in the air, not fully understanding what was happening. "Why do you have a gun? And why are you pointing it at me? I was gonna split the money with you." Willy's hands shook.

"Money?" Terry spat with disdain. "You think I want money? My family has even more money than yours."

"You're a terrorist?" Willy was sweating now.

"Oh, for cryin' out loud! Just because I have dark skin, you think I'm a terrorist? I'm not even religious at all. My adopted parents are super liberal atheists. We've talked about that." Terry thought for a moment, then walked toward Willy. "You know what? That is why I'm doing this! We've been roommates for two years, and you don't know I'm an atheist! You don't know that my dad is a billionaire. You probably didn't even know I was adopted. Like every other person on this planet, you think only about yourself. Well, that's going to change starting from today."

Terry reached behind Willy and withdrew the syringe filled with the liquid they had injected the mice with. Willy winced as he brought it around to show him.

"Come on, Terry, this is gettin' serious man," Willy advised, his voice shaking.

Terry stuck the small pistol in the middle of Willy's abdomen and fired. Willy folded in on himself and fell forward.

"See, that's why I used a small caliber. Hardly made a sound in your thick middle."

Willy held his hand in front of his face and looked at the dark blood. "You hit an artery," he croaked weakly. It was an odd observation, he knew, but it was all he could think of.

"Yeah, you'll bleed to death in a few minutes," Terry observed snarkily. "But your heart will pump long enough," Terry paused and bent down, sticking the needle into Willy's arm and pumping a few milliliters into him. "To spread the infection."

"I don't understand," Willy cried. "We were friends...."

"No, you used me. Just like my parents used me as their token adopted brown kid. Just like girls used me for my money and never gave me anything. I'm done being used and I'm changing the paradigm."

"Please, Terry," Willy pleaded, his voice losing steam.

Terry stuck the needle into his own arm and deposited a few milliliters. "If it's any consolation, a lot more are going to join you. Even me, before long. I'm booked on a jet to Atlanta International that leaves in an hour. That's the busiest airport in the country. I've got a two-hour layover there. Imagine how many people I'll infect. Then, I'm off to LaGuardia in New York and finally Heathrow in London. I'll probably die on the flight to London, but I'll infect everyone on the plane and the clean-up crew. Since it's airborne, they'll infect millions more. Who knows? Maybe everyone will die. Wouldn't that be something?"

Terry sat the gun on the table and started loading the petri dished into the boxes. "I'm going to dump these samples in the trash on the way to the airport. I've got our notebooks, too. No one will be able to replicate our work and no one will know who created it. Sorry, Willy, you're not going to be famous. Except maybe as Patient Zero." Terry laughed as he walked out of the room, boxes of samples under his arm. Had he turned around, he might have noticed the dead mouse was no longer lying in the puddle of blood.

CHAPTER 1

Donna sat in the passenger seat of the small SUV and touched her forehead with the back of her hand.

"I think the fever is breaking," she said. "Maybe we should go back to the hotel. I hate to cut our first family vacation short."

"It's not our first family vacation," her husband, Don, corrected her from the driver seat.

"Our first one in California," she noted.

"We've lived here six months. It's not like we're tourists on a timetable. We're not going anywhere, and neither is the Beach."

"I know that, Nod. I just wanted more time with my family at the beach."

"See, you're getting angry. And you're always angry when you're sick."

"Why do you call daddy Nod, mommy? I forget." The voice from the backseat belonged to their two-year-old daughter, Dorothy.

"Mommy always hated that we were 'Don and Donna'. She said it sounds like a lounge act. So, she calls me 'Nod' instead."

"What's a 'lounge act'?" the girl asked.

"Honey, you want to take this one?" Don suggested.

"Let's, uh, just stay quiet for a few minutes, okay honey? Mommy is getting a headache." Donna rubbed her temples, throwing back her long, dark curls.

"Okay, mommy," Dorothy stage whispered from behind.

They drove in silence along Hwy 46, the main artery between the San Joaquin Valley and the Central Coast. This was only the second time they had driven it, counting the trip over a few days ago. Most of the two-hour drive was miles and miles of open land. Some land was used for farming, some for cattle and some for oil. Don hated it, being born and raised in the 'metropolis' of Portland.

They had left Paso Robles over an hour ago and were, by Don's estimation, literally in the middle of nowhere. Some of his neighbors had told him this was a busy road, but both on the way over and the trip back had seen little traffic.

Don knew they should have called off the trip themselves due to the current 'Superbug' outbreak, but Dorothy and Donna would have been crushed. Besides, there hadn't been any reports of the illness in California four days ago when they left home, and he had a feeling the numbers were an exaggeration. And the reports of 'zombie-like' behavior were patently unbelievable. Still, when Donna started complaining of a fever an hour ago, he decided it would be prudent to head home.

Outside was a bright June day. The temperature, according to the car's dashboard thermometer, was only ninety degrees. He had been told this was unseasonably cool for this time of year.

The young family had relocated from Portland, Oregon to Bakersfield six months earlier so that Donna could take a position at the University. She had completed her doctorate in History four years ago and had been working as a post-doc when she was offered the professorship. Don, who wrote technology-related articles online part-time and took care of Dorothy full-time, pushed her to take her dream job even though they would be 'surrounded by gun nuts and religious freaks' in Bakersfield.

After coming over a rise in the road, Don saw an accident on the road a couple of miles in front of them. He was about to say something when he glanced over to Donna and saw her eyes closed. Not wanting to wake her, he continued forward.

There was a large semi-truck without a trailer and what looked like a minivan sticking out from under the front of the truck. It appeared to Don that the van crossed the dividing line and hit the truck head on. There was smoke but no fire. He didn't see anyone walking around.

"Ooh, that's bad," he mumbled to himself.

What followed happened very quickly. He walked slowing to the car, but a lone figure ran out of the wreckage and straight at their car. Don could see it was a woman. Her clothes were burned, torn, and she was covered in blood. One arm hung uselessly at her side as she pumped the other one furiously at a full sprint. Her face was contorted in what Don first thought was pain. A few steps closer and he realized she was angry.

He took his foot off the gas just as Donna coughed. It started as a couple of quick throat clearings and built to a fusillade of deep, guttural squeals. An avalanche of blood erupted from her mouth. nose, and her body bent nearly double with the attack.

The suddenness of the attack caused Don to swerve, but he caught the wheel and righted the SUV a moment before the runner slammed into the windshield. Don overcorrected and the car flipped over sideways. Time seemed to slow for Don as the car repeatedly rolled over. He could hear the runner's angry yelling, her body stuck halfway through the windshield. He could hear his wife's strained vomiting in the passenger seat as she sprayed blood everywhere. And he could hear his daughter's high-pitched screaming from the back seat.

The car continued rolling for what seemed like hours. When it finally stopped, it came to rest on the driver side. Once Don's vision cleared, he saw the runner was no longer moving. Her body had been cut nearly in half by the windshield. The angry look was forever etched into her face.

He glanced over to Donna. She hung limply, her seatbelt mostly holding her in place. She was covered in her own chunky blood. Her body twitched slightly as her vacant eyes stared at him.

His mind finally catching up to his eyes, he scrambled to turn and check on Dorothy. He had to take his seatbelt off to twist enough and his clumsiness slowed him down. When he finally got loose, he found her still strapped tightly in her car seat. Her eyes were open, and her head was locked at an unnatural angle.

Don scrambled to get to the backseat. He kept her belted in as he removed the entire car seat and exited the car through the broken sunroof. He was as gentle as he could be with her, but part of him knew it was too late.

He got just a few steps from the car before he sat the seat down and carefully removed her from it. He had no medical training, but her broken neck was obvious. Laying her body on the road, he checked for a heartbeat and found none. He performed CPR, but the grinding t under his hands when he started compressions caused him to quickly withdraw, afraid he would somehow cause her pain.

He stared down at her broken body, mentally tracing every edge of her face. The image he saw kept shifting from Dorothy to Donna and back. Ahigh pitch noise built up in his head, like a tea kettle about to sing. Then a pop came that radiated from his head down to his chest, and Don knew something inside his mind had broken.

Don heard footsteps on the road quickly approaching him. He paid them no attention as he continued to focus on his daughter's lifeless form. The footsteps slowed as they reached him.

"Was she sick?" came a man's gentle voice.

Don didn't respond.

"Is there anyone else in the car?" the voice continued.

Don nodded faintly.

The footsteps quickly moved toward Don's car. Don looked back to see a man peeking in through the sunroof. He heard a hushed 'Dear Lord' come from inside, then the man pulled back out. He walked around the wreck to look at the runner's body whose bottom half was sticking out of the windshield. He then returned to Don.

The man bent down to look at Dorothy. His eyes seemed to scan every part of her, like he was trying to memorize her features. The man had dark skin with a greying short beard and moustache and short grey hairs poking out from under his blue ball cap. His eyes flittered to Don.

"How 'bout you?" the man asked. "How're you feelin'?"

Surprisingly, Don didn't feel anything. He inadvertently flexed various muscles and just felt some tightness. He didn't reply.

"That's my truck over there. I saw the van swerving a little coming this way and as I got to it, it swerved right at me. The lady that ran at you kept trying to get into my truck, but she was too wild. Just bangin' her hands on the door until her shoulder came out of its socket. She couldn't even climb up. I think she had the sickness."

"Sickness?" Don asked absently.

"Haven't you been watchin' the news?" the older man asked incredulously.

"It's just a bug," Don answered without taking his eyes off Dorothy.

"It's worse than that. I've been following this closely for the last few weeks. They think it's an airborne virus. Worse than rabies! It either kills you or turns you into some kinda mindless, crazy monster. They freak out and try to kill everyone they see. It's all over the internet."

The fog in Don's brain slowly lifted. In truth, he and Donna hadn't been watching the news or surfing the internet a whole lot lately. Other than submitting an article a month ago, he hadn't really been on the internet much.

"I didn't know it was so bad," Don relented. "My wife was feverish. We were trying to get home. The lady just ran at us, hit the windshield."

"I'm so sorry," the man stated sheepishly. "I tried calling 911. It just rang and rang. My cell phone and CB are workin' fine. There's just no one to answer. I think we're on our own out here." The man paused, then continued. "My name's Al, by the way."

Don didn't care about names. He'd lost any care about his own life when that car rolled over. He replied absently, "My name's Nod."

CHAPTER 2

"We should probably bury them here," Al suggested.

The two men spent over an hour removing bodies from the wreckage. There were five altogether, including Donna, Dorothy, the runner, a man, and a small boy. They assumed the three were a young family. Though the bodies were mangled badly, they were intact. They laid them out on the side of the road underneath the only tree for miles.

"Here? On the side of the road?" Nod asked indignantly. He sat down in the dirt by his family, straightening Donna's long hair.

"No, we can move them a-ways off. Find a nice spot with soft dirt. I've got a folding shovel in my rig." Al paused for a moment, then continued. "Nod, man, I know what you've lost, believe me. But you've got to try and focus. Your girls would want you to keep goin'. We don't have a way to transport them and nowhere to transport them to."

"I'm not going anywhere," Nod stated matter-of-factly.

"You can't stay here, man. There's no food or water, except what's in our cars. Tomorrow is supposed to over a hundred. We can't survive in that kinda heat out here for very long."

Nod thought for a moment and replied, "I don't want to survive. If you want to go, then go."

Al was silent for a few minutes. "Listen, I'm going to find a spot to bury the others." He went to his truck and got the folding shovel, then trudged off into the wide-open space covered in short, dry grasses and sparse small brush.

Nod continued straightening Donna's hair and clothes, then did the same for Dorothy. When he was satisfied, he sat at their feet and wept into his pulled-up knees. He lost track of time but knew it had been awhile when he heard Al's footsteps again.

Al sucked in air and was covered in sweat. "I dug two large holes. We can put the family into one and your girls into another."

"I told you, I'm not going anywhere," Nod stated without looking at him.

Al took his hat off and ran his fingers through his curly, graying hair. He exhaled sharply, then pulled his wallet out of his back pocket. He unfolded it and pulled out an old picture.

"Take a look at this," he instructed, putting the picture in front of Nod's face. He glanced at it, then did a double take.

"Yours?" he asked.

"Sharon, my youngest."

"Looks like an old picture," Nod observed.

"She died shortly after this picture was taken twenty years ago. She was only six."

"I'm sorry," Nod said, his words ringing hollow.

"We were hit by a drunk coming home from visiting my in-laws. T-boned my car. She died instantly. My wife still has a big scar on her forehead. I didn't get a scratch. Luckily, my other four kids stayed with my in-laws."

"Sounds like you have a large family. You should get to them."

"I will, but the reason I showed you the picture is to let you know I do understand what you're feeling right now. I blamed myself. Spent months in a bottle. Nearly raised my hand to my teenaged son when he confronted me about it."

"Is that what fixed you?" Nod asked concerned.

"No, I got piss drunk again. Blacked out. Then, Sharon came to me in a dream. She talked to me. Told me everything I needed to hear. I sobered up after that." Al stared at the picture and then put it back in his wallet. "I know it was probably my own conscience and not Sharon, but it worked."

"Al, I can't just leave them here. And besides, I've got nowhere to go. No family here. What few friends I've made are not close. I barely even met my neighbors."

"You know me, now. We can stick together, help each other out."

"No, I'm just going to stay here. But I want you to go. Get to your family before it's too late." Nod's tone was almost pleading.

Al cast his eyes downward. "Okay, man, but I'm not going to leave you empty handed." Al went to his truck and returned a few minutes later. He was carrying a backpack and a few water bottles.

"I left some supplies in my rig. There's half a case of water bottles, a few cans of food and a small one-burner camp stove. Some other stuff that might help. You can stay in the sleeper cab, too." He motioned to his backpack. "I got everything I need for a week in this pack. Shouldn't take me but a few days to get home to Wasco."

Nod looked up at him and managed a weak smile. He saw a pistol in a drop holster on his right side that wasn't there before. "Good luck to you, Al. I hope your family is OK." He stuck out his hand.

Al took his hand and shook it but didn't let go. "I left directions to my house on a map in my rig. If you change your mind, come find me. Remember, you can honor their death by living your life." Al turned his hand so that Nod could see the word 'Sharon' tattooed on the inside of his wrist. "Good luck, Nod. I hope to see you again." He released Nod's hand and turned, walking east.

Al walked away until he disappeared over a rise. Though the land was wide open, there were a lot of small hills and gullies washed out from intermittent hard rain. He scanned the area for a few more minutes, somehow seeing the beauty in it for the first time.

He dragged the bodies of the other family to the holes Al had dug. It was only a hundred feet off the road and the bodies didn't weigh much. He found one hole was slightly bigger and assumed this was for the other family. It was just longer than the man's body and around four feet deep.

After he had positioned all three in the hole, he used the folding shovel to fill the hole back in. It took him the better part of an hour and he marveled at how strong Al must have been to dig both holes out by himself.

When he was finished, there was a mound a foot tall on top of the burial site. He gathered some fist-sized stones and placed them on top in the shape of a cross. Then he returned to the bodies of his family.

Coming out of the brush, he saw a large, dark bird land next to Dorothy's body. It surprised him and he didn't respond until he saw it peck at her arm.

"Hey!" Nod yelled, beginning to run and wave his arms. "Get away from her!"

The bird took off clumsily. *It wasn't a buzzard*, he thought. At least it didn't look like the buzzards on TV. Still, he knew that he had to bury them now before other things came looking for a meal.

He picked up Donna first. She was covered in blood, and it got all over him as they walked. He didn't care. If it was as contagious as he had heard, he was already infected.

He sat her body gently into the hole, then did the same with Dorothy. He spent several minutes arranging their bodies and settled on a warm embrace. If not for all the blood, they looked to be sleeping peacefully, as he had found them many times before. Nod felt the need to lay down next to them but resisted since he knew he needed to get them covered before he started feeling symptoms and lost his strength. Soon, he thought.

Nod shoveled the dirt into the hole, careful not to cover their faces until the last minute. Once the dirt spilled onto their faces, he worked more quickly. Soon, there was another mound of dirt. He placed another cross made of stones on top.

He walked back to their wrecked SUV and searched for one of the water bottles they had with them. He found one, an energy bar, and consumed both. The shoveling had severely dehydrated him and the small amount of food filled his belly. He knew it was a waste since he would be dead soon, but he needed the energy for one last job.

As he turned to go back to the grave site, he grabbed a blanket his daughter would use when she got cold on car trips. It was covered in cartoon rabbits, just like her room and most of her clothes. She was a big fan of rabbits.

Nod began digging a hole right next to his girls. Once Donna got feverish, she was dead in about an hour. He couldn't tell if he had a fever yet because he was so hot and dehydrated from all the work. If his grave wasn't dug quickly, he might not be able to do it.

Once the hole was three feet deep and long enough for him to lay in a fetal position, he stopped. The sun was going down now, leaving long shadows around him. His smartwatch showed it was nearly 6PM. He took one last look at the beautiful desolation, then crawled into the hole with the blanket and used the shovel to cover his legs and upper body with dirt. He wrapped the blanket around his head and shoulders, then did his best to burrow his arms under the dirt.

Nod knew this would not prevent a scavenger from finding his remains, but he hoped it would slow them down. Maybe by the time they sniff him out his body would be too desiccated for them to mess with. It didn't matter that much since he would be dead and beyond worry. Hopefully, he would see his girls again soon.

His forehead was warm followed by his cheeks. The sweat soaked into the blanket gave him some solace, knowing that it would be over soon. Within an hour or so, he would vomit his guts up and a few minutes later, he would be dead. Considering how tired he was, he hoped he would drift off soon and sleep through the whole thing. His eyes fixed on one of the rabbits on the blanket and he stared at it. Soon, his breathing slowed, and he got his wish to sleep.

CHAPTER 3

Nod woke. That was his first surprise. The blanket was still wrapped around his head, so he was very disoriented. Most of his body was still buried in the soft dirt of his shallow grave. He could tell even through the blanket that it was dark outside now. He couldn't have slept too long, he thought.

Nod's second surprise came when he realized he wasn't feverish. In fact, other than a pain in his back from lying in the dirt, he felt fine. He flexed his muscles under the dirt and confirmed that there were no aches or pains that weren't there after the accident.

"What the heck?" he whispered. He had a lifelong habit of thinking out loud. "I should be just as sick as Donna by now. We've been together non-stop for the last four days, sharing food, drinks and a bed. We had sex twice. I have to be infected." He lay there a while, perplexed at his continued good health.

Nod's third surprise came in the form of noise coming from the road. There were footsteps, glass being stepped on, metal being scraped. It sounded like someone or something was going through the wrecked vehicles. As far as he was concerned, they could have whatever they found.

At first, he thought it might be a person, but then he heard some low growling, too. *Coyotes*, he thought. Would they sniff him out and attack?

"Damn!" he whispered. As much as he wanted to die, the idea of being ripped apart by coyotes didn't appeal to him at all. He slowly moved his arms until they were free, then pulled the blanket from his head. It was dark, but there was some light from the crescent moon and stars. Moving slowly and deliberately, he slid the dirt off his body until he could move his legs, then rolled onto his knees, and looked toward the cars.

It was too dark to see much more than outlines. He didn't hear anything now and couldn't make out any moving shapes. He scanned up and down the road, but he couldn't see anything moving.

Something hit him hard from the side, rolling him over. Nod cried out, surprised and hurt. The attacker snarled and grabbed at him. He reacted by curling up and trying to roll away, but the attacker was vicious, pummeling Nod and scratching at him. It tore at his clothes. There didn't seem to be any design to the attack, just brutality.

Nod tried to move away, but the predator grabbed at him any way it could. It tried biting through his pants leg, but the tough denim resisted the animal's bite. Nod's hand pulled at the dirt until it found something solid: the folding shovel.

Nod knew exactly what it was as soon as his hand curled around it. He gripped it hard and swung back at his attacker. It found something hard because it 'klang'-ed loudly and the animal released its grip for just a second.

Nod pulled his legs away and stood up. The dark figure growled as it rolled and began to rise. He could see now that his attacker was a person. It reached quickly for him, letting out a vicious roar. Nod delivered another blow to the side of its head. It went down on one knee, and Nod continued striking it until his blows were met with only moist resistance.

When he realized the person wasn't moving, he stepped back. He still held the small shovel up with one hand, ready to strike. But the form on the ground didn't move.

Nod slowly brought the shovel down and looked a little closer at his attacker. It was a man, slightly taller than him. He tapped his smartwatch and turned on the flashlight app, then shined it at the man on the ground. Bending down to see more clearly, he suddenly recoiled in horror. The face, now frozen and contorted with anger, belonged to Al.

Nod sat hard on the mound of dirt next to his grave. It was Al, and he was dead. He worked the situation over and over in his head and realized Al must have been infected. He had the same look on his face that 'the runner' had earlier.

"Did we infect him?" Nod whispered. "Did he get infected moving the bodies? Or was he already infected and didn't know it?"

Nod glanced at his smartwatch. It was almost 5AM. Al would have left almost twelve hours ago. Plenty of time for him to develop a fever and go nuts.

"Dang it, Al," Nod murmured. "I really hoped you'd see your family again." The shovel dropped to the dirt. Realizing he was sitting on top his family's grave, he quickly shot up. He dusted his pants off as if removing the dirt would somehow make it OK to have sat there. He fixed the stone cross that his backside had knocked askew.

"So now I've lost my family and my soul," Nod huffed. "But apparently I want to live. Or I'm too big a coward to die."

He looked over at Al's body. The growing light in the east wasn't enough to see everything yet, but he noticed the outline of the holster still on his hip. He shined his smartwatch light in that direction and saw the pistol was still there.

"Well, a new opportunity," Nod exhaled. He reached for the pistol and found it stuck. Looking more closely, he saw there was a small leather snap holding it in place. He unsnapped it and withdrew the large gun.

Nod had never held a real gun in his life, much less fired one. He hated guns. Feared them, really. He had no idea what kind of pistol it was or the kind of bullets it used. It was lighter than he expected. He knew it wasn't a revolver since it didn't have the cylinder in the middle. Maybe a Glock? Nod had heard that term before, but he didn't know if that was a caliber or a brand name.

This was his way out. If he shot himself in the head, it would be quick and painless. Unless he screwed it up, he thought. He pointed the gun in the direction of the rising sun and pulled the trigger.

Nothing happened. The trigger wouldn't press. Was it broken? Was it jammed? "The safety!" he yelped. "The safety's on. How do you turn it off?" He examined the pistol until he found a large switch near the back and turned it. There was also a lever on the back of the handle that would depress when he gripped it. Maybe a second safety?

Nod pointed the gun again and pulled the trigger. This time it fired, and it nearly jumped out of his hand. It wasn't as loud as he expected, but it echoed for miles. Gripping it tighter, he pulled the trigger again. This time went much smoother.

"Alright, that should do it," Nod sighed quietly. He sat next to the mound of dirt that covered his family's bodies. "God, forgive me," he whispered, then put the barrel just above his right ear. He closed his eyes gently and slowly began to tighten his trigger finger.

Movement in the grass next to him caught his attention. He looked to his left and saw a rabbit chewing on a small plant. It was only a few feet away and stared at him as it chewed.

Nod froze. It looked like a cottontail, Dorothy's favorite kind of rabbit. The same kind that adorned the blanket he had used to wrap his head the day before. He slowly lowered the pistol as he focused. Pulling a tuft of green grass, he held it out to the rabbit who hopped over and started munching on it.

"Did she send you?" Nod asked quietly. The rabbit continued munching. "Is she watching? Dorothy, can you hear me?" His voice was getting louder. He pulled more grass and offered it to the rabbit who was happy to have it.

"I miss you and mommy, honey so much." He watched the rabbit for any sign of recognition. Nod's mind raced. "Am I crazy? I know something happened when you died. Something inside my mind just snapped."

The rabbit stopped eating and hopped closer to Nod. It still looked around nervously, but it inched closer to Nod's leg. It stopped just below his knee, then seemingly rested its head there.

Tears rolled down his eyes. He gently placed his hand on top of the rabbit's head and stroked it. To his surprise, the rabbit let him. "I love you, Dorothy."

As if on cue, the rabbit looked away. Then it quickly hopped a few feet away. Its head jotted back and forth, then another larger rabbit joined it.

"Donna?" Nod asked. The large rabbit looked back at him. The two began to hop away gingerly. Nod quickly stood up and tried to follow.

"Wait!" he yelled. The rabbits disappeared into the grass as Nod scrambled to get to them. When he caught up, they were nowhere to be seen. However, Dorothy's blanket, which he had thrown off earlier, was lying there among the dry grass. He picked it up and walked back to where he had been sitting.

"Alright ladies, I can take a hint," he said loudly. "I'm not giving up. I'll do my best to survive, for now. I don't know how long I can make it on my own, but I promise you I won't kill myself. I just need to figure out what to do." He still had the pistol in his hand and tried to put it in his pocket, but it was too big to fit comfortably. Remembering where he got it, he went to Al's body and took off his belt and holster. He secured the belt around his waist and put the pistol in the holster.

Since Al still wore his backpack, he took that, too, and, searching his pockets, found an old pocketknife. At some point, he noticed the blue ball cap was missing. When his search was complete, he dragged Al's body into the grave he had dug for himself and covered him up.

"I think he was a good man, ladies. He tried to help me. He'll help you if he can." He paused for a moment. "Rest in peace, Al. Give Sharon a big hug from me. And please look after my girls."

He gathered his items and walked back to his wrecked SUV. He searched the inside for items he might need. The luggage had spilled open in the roll over, so it took a while to find all his clothes scattered around the cargo area. His soft suitcase lay open, but the bag containing his toiletries was strapped inside. He put his clothing back inside as neatly as he could.

He searched Donna's suitcase to find her toiletry bag and even took the one from Dorothy's. Her toothpaste may have tasted and smelled like bubblegum, but it still worked. And her little toothbrush was brand new.

They had stopped and bought a few bottles of water and some protein bars before they left. There was also a bag of corn chips. All these things, along with Dorothy's blanket, he brought to Al's rig and sat them by the door.

Nod checked the minivan for anything useful, but the inside was a mess. It had taken him and Al quite a while to get the bodies of the man and boy out. Everything was bent from the impact and there was no luggage or anything else useful that he could find. They must have been in a hurry, Nod assumed.

Al's rig was next. He opened the driver side and crawled in. Pictures of his family covered the dash. He moved to the sleeper cab. The opening faced the sunrise, so he could see fairly well. There was a comfortable mattress with blankets. A dozen or so water bottles were lined up along the edge. There was a can of chili beans and a can of ravioli. In the corner was a small, one-burner stove and the smallest propane bottle Nod had ever seen.

He crawled back into the driver seat. There was a road atlas in the passenger seat. The page was open to Wasco, CA and an address was written on it. Al really had left directions to his house.

After searching around the cab, he found a small first aid kit and a long flashlight. The flashlight was bright, but heavy. The first aid kit had a few upgrades like gauze and extra athletic tape.

Nod gathered all the supplies he found and placed them on the ground near the rig in the shade. Then he laid out the contents of Al's backpack. He found a box of bullets labeled .45 ACP and a spare magazine that appeared to fit the pistol. The box of one hundred was about half full and the magazine was topped off. Remembering what he'd seen playing *Call of Duty*, he practiced loading and unloading the pistol.

Other than the bullets, there wasn't a whole lot. A few more water bottles. an extra pair of socks, a black hoodie, and a single energy bar. Al had said he had enough supplies in his backpack to last a week. What Nod found wouldn't' last more than a day. He had left the other supplies for Nod knowing he would be very thirsty and very hungry by the time he got home. Or maybe Al knew he would never make it home. Either way, it was another selfless act.

Altogether, he had three days of food if he rationed well. Probably no more than four- or five-days' worth of water if it got as hot as Al had said.

"Now what?" Nod asked himself. "Go home or stay here and hope someone comes along? Or trek back to Paso Robles? Maybe the military was setting up a relief station or something. There were tons of military vehicles on the 101. If only I had internet access."

CHAPTER 4

Nod slapped his forehead. "Some techie I am," he growled to himself. He searched his pockets and didn't find his cell phone. Remembering his and Donna's cell phones were both on charging cradles when the accident happened, he jogged back to the SUV wreckage to search for them.

The sun was up above the hills now, so he could see better. He found his phone first and unfortunately it was bent nearly in half. He sighed but had the presence of mind to remove the memory card and battery. Since he and Donna had bought the same model of cell phone, he knew the battery should work in both.

It took fifteen minutes to find Donna's phone. It had bounced under her seat and rested there. Nod was relieved to see the screen was not cracked and it looked to be in decent shape. The bright pink case and silver dangles were unmarred. He hit the side button and the home screen came up.

"Yes!" he exclaimed. Then he noticed there was no internet connection and was crushed. Reception had been spotty on the road and they had lost satellite radio coverage several times on the trip over. He figured he might be able to get reception later in the day or if he climbed the tall hill east of the rig.

Al had said he checked his phone and CB after the accident. Nod had seen the CB radio installed underneath the dash, just like in the movies. But he hadn't noticed a cell phone in the cab or when he had checked Al's body before burial.

"It must still be in the truck," Nod determined. He went back to the cab and searched again, finding nothing new. He sat in the driver seat and drummed his hands on the steering wheel. On second thought, he knew there was no way Al would have left it in the cab when he started home.

An image of Al walking home crept into Nod's mind. Perhaps Al was checking for a connection or trying to reach someone on the phone as he wiped his feverish brow. Then the vomiting started, and Al probably doubled over, dropping the phone. He imagined it still there on the road, somewhere, many miles east. Maybe it was ringing, over and over.

Nod gathered up his provisions and placed them in the rig. He wasn't too worried about thieves, but he decided it would be best to have everything squirreled away in the same place in case he needed to hunker down for some reason.

Nod decided it was time to climb the tall hill and attempt to get cell reception. He grabbed a water bottle and the bag of corn chips and climbed down onto the road. The keys were still in the ignition, so he debated whether or not to lock the doors. In the end, he left then open just in case he had to get back inside in a hurry.

The base of the hill was about a quarter of a mile from the road. He couldn't tell how tall it was, but the climb wasn't too hard. Luckily, he was in decent shape and used to long walks. It took him ten minutes to reach the top, where he found a small cluster of oak trees.

He checked the screen again and found three bars. Good enough for a decent connection, he thought. Scanning the area, he saw the top of the hill was roughly the size and shape of a football field with an even gentler slope on the back size. It looked like a well-worn dirt road led up there and several old fire pits dotted the area.

"Someone's vacation spot," he chuckled to himself. And he had to admit, it was a nice view. Though it was desolate as far as he could see, the view was obstructed in most directions after a few miles. They had passed large vineyards to the west and they had seen a few signs on the highway that indicated directions to nearby small towns. So, he knew there might be others within walking distance. This thought made him feel slightly less lonely.

"The Land of Nod," he whispered as he surveyed the area. He knew about the Land of Nod mentioned in the Bible. It was where Cain was exiled to after killing his brother, Abel. He wondered if this is what Cain must have felt like, being sent out into the wilderness when only a handful of people were even alive. It was a loneliness that can't be described but certainly Cain must have felt it, too. Nod was starting to think the Bible wasn't just a collection of stories and maybe it was some kind of message from God, a way to prepare us for our own ignorance.

The reflection didn't last long, though. Seeing the 'girlie' pink cell phone cover brought his deep sadness back as it cascaded to the front of his mind. They had bought their cell phones at the same time and on the same plan. They got the phones for free with the caveat that they had to get the same model. Not wanting to get them mixed up, Donna bought the most 'girlie' phone case she could find. It was bright pink with sparkles and had silver charms hanging off of one corner. Nod had gone for the thick gun-metal gray cover that screamed 'manliness.'

He was glad Donna hadn't done the 'typical mom' thing and used a picture of Dorothy as her background. He would look at the pictures later, when he was feeling a little stronger, but for now he needed to focus.

Nod spent fifteen minutes trying every contact in Donna's phone. He tried 911 first, and it just rang and rang. Then he moved on to family, friends, colleagues, and then finally businesses. The phone at her gynecologist's office clicked as if someone answered, but all Nod heard was the growling of a 'wild animal' in the background. The 'wild animal' sounded a lot like Al had that morning.

Outside of voicemail, no other line was picked up. Nod then tried calling every phone number he could remember. No one picked up.

Next Nod went to the internet. He spent several hours surfing various news websites. Many of the US-based sites had not been updated in twenty-four hours. Most of the international sites were still updating regularly, but the news was dwindling.

In short, the United States, and most other western countries, were no longer functioning. Government sources had determined the outbreak started in the US but had spread worldwide within a week. Bedlam had broken out as rogue countries tried to use the chaos to settle ancient scores. Armies had been on the march until infections stopped them in their tracks. Several nuclear warheads had been detonated in the middle east and eastern Europe.

Australia was the last country with no reported infections and had closed their borders. Aircraft were not allowed to enter their airspace and ships were not allowed with a hundred nautical miles. There were unconfirmed reports of passenger aircraft being shot down by the Australian Air Force and approached cruise ships being sunk by the Australian Navy.

The infection had been initially identified as an Ebola-like filovirus. Within days of identification, the CDC reported it was likely a man-made virus as DNA testing had identified genes from the common flu virus and rabies. Given the varied hotspots of infection spanning the globe, it was considered an act of terrorism. However, no terrorist organizations had taken responsibility.

The infection cycle was at least partially worked out. The virus was airborne and blood borne. There were reports of people becoming infected who hadn't left their homes in a week causing speculation that the virus could travel over distances by wind. Once a person was infected, they culd infect others within the hour. The first symptoms were seen in five to eight hours. Death by system collapse generally happened within one to two hours of symptoms presenting themselves.

Death rates were staggering. Over sixty percent of those infected died outright. No successful treatment had been found. Very few labs were even operating anymore to test new treatments.

Even more alarming, about thirty percent of those infected went insane following a partial system collapse. Survivors became not unlike dogs with advanced rabies. They become hyperactive, unable to slow down. They attack and kill anything moving, including, at times, other infected. They appear to be fueled by epinephrine and rage.

What Nod read next chilled him to the core. It was expected that less than ten percent, maybe as little as one percent, of the population was immune to the disease and immunity tended to be genetic. There were multiple reports where half of a family died while the other half never even got sick. Donna was sick, but Dorothy had no symptoms whatsoever. Had there been no accident, she might still be alive. That revelation caused him to break down again.

A high-pitched whine of a vehicle brought him out of his morose. He scanned the area, wiping his eyes, and saw a military vehicle on the highway coming from the west, maybe five miles away. It moved fast, but he was sure he could get to the road before it passed by.

Nod sprinted toward the edge of the slope, sticking the phone in his pocket. He left the water and corn chips behind, not thinking of them. When he got to the edge of the downward slope, he slowed, but still hurried. Every few steps, he would look up to see the vehicle a little closer.

When he reached the bottom, the vehicle was only half a mile away. He waved his hands in the air, trying to get the driver's attention. The vehicle, which appeared to Nod to be a Humvee, barely slowed as it swerved to miss Nod's overturned SUV. When it got to the rig and van wreckage, it had to slow to go off the shoulder and to get around it. It was then Nod saw that the driver wasn't dressed like a soldier, though he wore a military-style gas mask.

As if just seeing Nod, the Humvee came to a full stop when it came around the larger wreckage. Nod saw a single person inside, a man most likely, looking at him. He got out with a large, black rifle in his hands. He came around the Humvee and pointed it at Nod.

Nod yelled, "Don't shoot!" as he threw his hands in the air.

The man, dressed in a blue t-shirt and jeans, stared at Nod. Finally, he asked, "Do you have any food or water?"

Nod could barely understand him through the gas mask. But he had a feeling the man wasn't offering food or water but looking for them. He slowly shook his head no.

The man was visibly sweated and nervously breathed hard through the filter. After a moment, he responded, "Well, I don't either. I'm…. sorry."

"Can you tell me what's happening?" Nod pleaded.

"The world's gone to Hell!" the man replied. "People are dyin' in the streets. Others are goin' crazy, killin' everything they see. It's like everything was okay, then everyone got sick all of a sudden. I think it's in the air. I was in Santa Barbara when it started and every time I would get to a new town, people were dyin'."

"Are you sick? Feverish?" Nod asked.

"Not yet. That's why I'm wearin' this mask. I'm tryin' to get to my family in Fresno." The man's hands tightened on the rifle as if remembering it was there. "Are you sure you don't have anything?"

"Everything I had died in that car," Nod replied, pointing to the SUV.

The man thought. "Well, I'm sorry to hear that. I guess you could ride with me to Fresno." The man's voice was unsteady, as if he wasn't sure he meant his words.

Nod thought for a moment. The man's offer could just be a ploy to get his meager supplies. Besides, Fresno was a large city and that seemed like the last place Nod would want to be.

"Thanks, I'm fine here."

"Are you sure?" the man asked, his voice sounding sincere. "Helps not comin'. I only got this Humvee because all of the military guys were dead. They tried to block the roads yesterday afternoon but started dyin' not long after."

"I'd rather be here, close to my family," Nod replied, pointing to the field.

The man stared to where Nod pointed. Realization of what Nod meant sat in. "Well, good luck to you." The man dropped the rifle down to his side and turned to get back into the Humvee.

"Wait!" Nod yelped.

The man turned. "Yeah?"

"The coast. How bad is it? Is anyone alive?"

"Just the Crazies running around. And there's a lot of 'em. I'd stay away if you can." With that, the man jumped back into the Humvee and sped around the rig. When he got a hundred or so feet away, he stopped and dropped something out of his door. The engine revved loudly, as if calling Nod's attention, then he took off again and was soon out of sight.

Nod approached where the Humvee had stopped cautiously. He paused a moment and thought about the word the man had used for the infected and decided 'Crazies' was a good name for them. He spied a large, black duffle bag as he neared. The top was unzipped, and he could see the barrel of a rifle pointing out of it. He grabbed the barrel and pulled out a rifle. Below that was at least a dozen magazines that appeared to be filled with bullets.

Nod stuffed the rifle back into the bag and took the handles. He picked it up and found it was much heavier than he expected. Walking back to the rig with it, he wondered why the guy had left it for him. "Maybe he was just a good guy and thought I could use it. Probably had that vehicle stuffed with guns and ammo for the trip," he mumbled to himself.

He hefted the heavy bag up into the rig and placed it in the floorboard on the passenger side. It took up too much space to fit in the sleeper cab with him. Besides, he knew even less about how to use the rifle than he did about the pistol.

It was starting to get hot in the truck, so he rolled the manual windows down most of the way. Then he grabbed a water bottle and made the trek back up to the top of the hill. He found his water bottle and unopened bag of chips right where he had left them.

Out of curiosity, he decided to see if there was any information about Portland. His parents had both died several years ago, but he had a sister and her family was still living there. If he was immune, she and her two kids might be, too. He had a few cousins living there and they might also be immune.

The last news he could find on Portland was from yesterday morning. The infection was there, and military had moved in to help. Sections of the city had been sealed, including the area his sister lived in.

Nod wished he could talk with her. It would really be nice to share his grief with someone. Maybe he could email her.

Nod slapped his forehead again. He was holding a cellphone in his hand lamenting that he couldn't talk to her. He searched Donna's contacts, hoping to find his sister listed. And there it was: Stella Douglas. He hit the call button.

At first, each ring built his anticipation. After four rings, it was the opposite. On the sixth ring, her voice mail answered. Sadly, it wasn't even her voice but that of a computer telling him to leave a message. Then came the beep.

"Stella," he began slowly. "I hope you, Dave, and the kids are okay. I'm sorry I haven't called in so long. You probably won't believe I'm sitting on a hill overlooking the most desolate part of California you could imagine. Maybe fifty miles from the coast, but it's really hot. Stella," Nod's voice caught in his throat. "Donna and Dorothy are dead. There was an accident. I don't want to relive it, but I can tell you they didn't suffer." Nod paused but remembered his recording time would be limited. "Stella, I don't know what I'm going to do. I'll probably stay in the area for a while. Maybe I'll find an empty house and gather food and stuff. Please, stay safe and call me if you can. I love you."

Nod pressed the 'End' button on the screen. Once again, he was racked with sorrow and wept bitterly. He knew that even if Stella and her kids were immune, there was still a lot of ways for them to die. He recited a silent prayer for them, something he hadn't done since he was a child.

CHAPTER 5

By nightfall, Nod was back in the rig. For now, he decided he wouldn't go anywhere. He told himself he was using the time to gain as much 'intelligence' as he could. But really, he didn't know what to do. He was happy to discover that he could plug the phone in to the charging port in the rig and it would charge it. He switched batteries in the phone to make sure both were fully charged for when the truck's battery eventually went dead.

The phone was important to him as a resource, but it was also what it contained. All of Donna's pictures and videos were on her SD card. His SD card also had lots of pictures and videos. That was all that remained of them. He didn't know anyone that made actual, physical photographs anymore. Heck, he didn't know anyone that even had regular camera.

To ensure something survived, he transferred all of Donna's media to the phone, then switched SD cards out and transferred his as well. Then, he transferred all the images and videos to both SD cards and left them on the phone. He also made sure he could get to the internet site they used to back up all those images and videos and was reassured that it was available for now.

He decided not to charge his smartwatch. He had found the charger unharmed in his suitcase, but he didn't want to waste the limited amount of juice in the rig's battery on it. Since it had been synced to his phone, which was destroyed, it was pretty much only good for telling time now and Donna's phone did that fine. There was nothing important stored on it either, so he would wear it until it ran out of power.

Nod spent several hours visiting websites that postulated and described end-of-the-world scenarios. There were thousands but he was able to narrow it down to a few that were useful. There was a lot of talk about learning to use guns, squirreling away supplies, setting up alternate power sources and creating a network of people with various skills. He hadn't done any of that and, frankly, only the gun practice would have helped him now.

A few websites were devoted to preparing for biological warfare, which seemed to match his current situation a little better. The author divided the event into two parts: Survival during the infection and survival post-infection.

Surviving during the infection meant finding a 'hidey-hole' and staying there until the initial die-off is over. Create sterile conditions if you need to venture out into the wilderness of medical waste. It seemed to Nod that this part of the outbreak was probably close to being over. The infection moved over the landscape like a wildfire instead of taking the many months the website had postulated.

The second part of the event, post-outbreak survival would be trickier. Even the author's wildest dreams hadn't played out a scenario where the survival rate was so low. They had electricity as well as food and running water. The power wouldn't last forever, though. Eventually components would wear out and break down. He was glad he wasn't near any large dams or nuclear power plants.

Of course, there were the infected survivors. While there were a lot of websites dealing with 'fictional' zombie-style apocalypses, these infected weren't much like their mindless, stumbling fictional counterparts. They weren't mindless, but single-minded. They wanted only to kill, according to the internet reports. And his experience with Al cemented that idea. Cause enough damage and they died, just like regular humans.

Nod used the calculator on the phone to do some math. There were forty million people in California. That means over twenty-four million people were dead or dying. Twelve million were crazed killers. And less than four million were likely immune and hopefully still alive. And that was the high estimate.

"How many were really alive, though?" he wondered aloud. "How many were killed by infected relatives or friends? How many just wanted to die, like me? There may be half that." Nod shuddered.

Nod looked at the time on his smartwatch, which he noted only had half its charge remaining. "Almost midnight," he whispered. "Guess I should get some sleep." He climbed into the cab to make sure the doors were locked, and the windows rolled up enough so someone couldn't reach in, then clicked the overhead light in the cabin off. He rolled the rabbit blanket up to use as a pillow. It still smelled like

Dorothy, which brought tears at first, then calmness. Soon he was asleep, a smile on his face.

***

Nod woke up to scratches and barking outside. The sun was up already, albeit still low over the hills. He checked his smartwatch and found it to be just after 7AM. He was starving and decided to eat a protein bar after he went outside and peed.

Then it registered that something, probably a dog, was outside. He peeked out of the sleeper and around the driver seat. Just then, the dog's face leapt up into the view on the other side of the window. It was snarling and foaming at the mouth.

Nod had never seen a rabid dog in real life, but he figured this was textbook. His research the day before had mentioned that animals other than mammals, like reptiles, fish and insects, were unaffected by the superbug. Mammals, on the other hand, had varied reactions. The closer an animal was genetically 'related' to humans, the worse the impact. Livestock were being wiped out with almost a ninety-percent death rate and no crazed infected. Pigs were at a similar death rate and a five percent crazed infected rate.

Dog infection rates were similar across all breeds since they were all the same species. The only information released about them showed most died outright within a few hours of contracting the virus. About ten percent took on the rabid symptoms and ten percent or so were immune.

Nod decided he needed a better name for the infected. 'Zombie' was too casual. 'Rabids' sounded like a cartoon Dorothy used to watch. Maybe 'Runners' since he used that term to refer to the lady that hit their windshield. He settled on 'infected'.

The dog's wet maw hitting the window hard brought Nod out of his thoughts. "Holy crap!" he exclaimed and fell back on his butt.

Nod had never been a dog lover, and this wasn't helping. A few more hits like that and the window might shatter. The head looked like a German Shepherd and he knew these dogs were used by police and military because they were very tough and agile. The virus only supercharged that. He needed to kill it.

The pistol had been sitting on the bed next to him. He had put the safety back on, so he didn't grab it in the middle of the night and accidentally shoot himself. There wasn't enough room to stick the gun outside the window to shoot the dog. And if he rolled it down anymore, the dog might be able to get his paws on it enough to break it.

He decided to be quick. Wait until the dog jumps up, then quickly roll the window down and fire before he jumps back up. And hope the bullet hits him.

Nod took several deep breaths and moved to the driver seat. The dogs' lunges were irregular and difficult to time. Then it dawned on Nod that if he bumped the door open as the dog jumped, it would knock him off the running board he was perched on and onto the ground. That would give him several more seconds to act.

Nod placed the safety in the 'off' position, then sat it in his lap. He unlocked the door and grabbed the handle. After waiting for a few more lunges, he pushed the door open about six inches as soon as the dogs' face was visible in the window. It pushed the animal off the running boards just as Nod had hoped. He then quickly cranked the handle on the window fast, moving the wrong direction first, then correcting and rolling it down. He leaned forward and stuck the pistol out of the window just as the dog's mouth grabbed it from the side and twisted it out of his hands. Nod marveled at its incredible speed.

No sooner had Nod registered what had happened when the animal's head returned to the window. Its renewed vigor had his paws on top of the glass and its head coming right at Nod's face. Nod leaped sideways toward the passenger seat, kicking at the dog's snout repeatedly. It was undeterred and continued slowly crawled inside.

As he scrambled to get away, Nod's right hand tangled in something in the floorboard. He turned and saw the duffel bag. "The rifle!" he screamed, suddenly remembering it existed. He clumsily rolled over and dug it out of the bag. He got it up just as half the dog's body struggled angrily through the opening. He only halfway aimed, then pulled the trigger. Nothing happened.

"Damn it!" he yelled. He searched for the safety and found it quickly. He pushed it off, then fired as the dog's mouth grabbed at the front of the barrel. Though he had only depressed the trigger once, it fired three times, piercing the dog's head twice. It slumped in the driver seat.

"Three round burst," Nod whispered as he breathed heavily. "That's cool." It dawned on him that he didn't hear his voice, only a loud ringing in his ears. It confused him, at first, then he realized he had fired in a confined area. He didn't notice how loud it was when he had fired because he was so scared. "I need some practice with this thing," he stated, staring at the long, black rifle in his hand.

A few minutes later, he had dragged the dog's body out of the rig and out into the scrub. Once he finished, he finally relieved himself. "I'm surprised I didn't pee my pants," he confessed, looking over at the animal. He was happy when he realized the ringing in his ears had stopped.

He went back to the rig and survey the damage. While two of the bullets had struck the dog and passed through the opening of the window, one bullet had passed through the door, shattering the window. That was problem since he knew there might be crazed animals out here now. Al had said the runner couldn't climb on his running board when she was trying to get to him, but the dog had no problem doing so. His agility didn't appear to be negatively impacted by the virus in any way. The opposite was true since he had recovered from his fall and jumped back up so quickly.

Nod knew he needed more practice with the rifle. Just like when he played video games, it was always better to practice with a weapon before you used it. He hadn't even realized that the switch on the side of the rifle, that he thought was the safety, also selected for a single shot, three round burst or fully automatic fire.

The problem was the noise. Practicing out in the open with the 'especially loud' rifle was bound to draw the attention of any crazed people or animals from miles away. It could be that the hills that dotted the area would make it hard to determine where the sound was coming from. And if he walked a couple of miles or so east, toward the lower population area, the chances of drawing anything would be a lot less.

He took the rifle and studied it. It was much heavier than he expected. The firing selector he was now familiar with. And there was a sling that would make it easier to carry long distances. He loaded and unloaded the magazine and put a new bullet in the chamber to make sure he knew how to do it. The old bullet popped out and he stuck it in his pocket. He decided to put the firing selector on single shot, so he didn't waste bullets.

Nod didn't want to carry the whole duffle bag stuffed with ammo, so he reached in and took out two spare magazines and put them in his back pockets. He assumed they each held thirty rounds, just like in *Call of Duty*, but he would go through them more thoroughly later.

He grabbed a full water bottle, a protein bar, and an empty water bottle to use as a target and took off east on the road. He held the rifle loosely in his hands, letting the sling put a lot of the weight on his shoulder. He didn't know if it was just instinctual now or if he had just seen it in so many movies, but he scanned the area from side to side suspiciously as he walked.

When he got to where he felt was a safe distance, he stopped and ate the protein bar. As he did, he looked for a suitable place for target practice off the road. It was breezy this morning, which felt good on his face, but it blew the short grasses and scrub brush around a lot. A couple of hundred yards away, he spotted a large rock sticking up over the scrub. He walked out to the rock and placed the empty water bottle on top. The slight breeze blew it off, so he scooped some dirt and put it in the bottle to give it some weight. The bottle held its place in the breeze, and he walked back about fifty paces.

There was a short scope on the rifle. He had seen the switch for it earlier and slid it to the 'on' position. A tiny red dot appeared in the middle when he looked through it. Again, just like *Call of Duty*. He set the red dot on the target and pulled the trigger. The rifle buck back hard, hitting his shoulder in the process.

"Damn!" he yelled, rubbing his shoulder. "That's gonna bruise."

He took aim again, having completely missed the target on his first try. This time he snugged the butt of the rifle up against his shoulder tightly. Putting the dot on the water bottle again, he squeezed the trigger. It struck the rock just under the bottle, spending sparks and rock chips into the air.

"OK," Nod told himself. "Remember to hold your breath this time. Squeeze, don't pull." His next shot knocked the bottle off the rock.

"Yes!" he cried out triumphantly. He trotted over to the rock and picked up the plastic bottle. The top of it had been ripped off with the bullet passing through it. Not really thinking about it, he searched for the missing top and found a dozen or so cans behind rock, each one peppered with bullet holes.

"I guess this is the place for practice," he said aloud, admiring the dark red patina from the old cans. He placed three of the cans and what was left of the water bottle on the rock again. He continued his practice, moving further and further away from his targets. Though he was by no means an expert, by the time he had worked through two magazines, he felt proficient and comfortable with the rifle. He had even taken some shots with the pistol and was happy with the results.

He walked back out to the road and started back to the rig. As he walked, he continued to scan his surroundings. Something caught his eye just off the road and he stopped and turned to look in that direction. The breeze was blowing things about, but he spotted it again. A patch of blue about thirty feet away. He walked toward it and was surprised when he finally realized what it was: Al's blue ball cap.

Nod stared at it and wondered why it was there. Maybe the wind, coming from the east had blown it this far or maybe he didn't lose it until he got this close. He wasn't sure, but he reached down and picked it up. He had assumed it was a Dodger's hat, but there wasn't anything identifying it as affiliated with the team. It was just a plain blue ball cap.

Nod put it on his head, then adjusted the band a little to fit him. He figured it would be good for keeping the sun off his close-cropped head. And it would remind him of Al, his continued benefactor even from the grave.

CHAPTER 6

Nod spent the rest of the day with various chores and exploring the area. He had gone through the duffle bag when he returned and found more than he had seen initially. There were twenty magazines, all filled except for the ones he used for practice. He was pleased to find boxes of ammunition marked '5.56' in the bottom of the bag and used them to refill the magazines he had used.

Also, in the duffle bag were six grenades. They were smaller than he expected, and he thought maybe they were smoke bombs. However, when he searched for them online, he found they were indeed explosive grenades.

The final thing he found in the bag was a set of binoculars. They were compact but heavy, which seemed to be standard for all military equipment, Nod thought. No bells and whistles, they just made far away objects closer.

In the afternoon, Nod climbed the tall hill with the binoculars. He took a water bottle and his pistol, which he decided he would take with him everywhere from now on. When he reached to top, he took his familiar spot under the tree and began scanning the distance with the binoculars.

"Just glassin'," he said with a chuckle, repeating a popular meme he had seen on the internet.

Toward the east was the 'Great Central Valley' and beyond that the Sierras. The hills and distance would obscure either of these, but he looked anyway. There was a rest stop, he remembered, maybe ten miles from where he was. Then came the Fresno turnoff followed by some larger hills. There was a small town not long before you reached I-5. He wasn't sure of any distances, but he knew it was over an hour in the car, so it would probably take some time, maybe days, to walk it. He could use the mapping app on Donna's phone if he felt the need.

His view south and north were completely obscured by mountains and haze. Probably smog to the south, since that was the direction of Los Angeles, he thought. And there was no way he could ever see himself venturing north, toward San Francisco or Sacramento, or south considering what those high population areas would be like now.

To the west was the small town of Paso Robles. Its biggest claim to fame was a State Fair every year, judging by the number of signs Nod had seen driving through. It was also where beach-bound folks from the Central Valley drove, before turning to head north or south along Highway 101. Either direction got you to the coast, apparently. Though the town was too far to see, Nod noticed a lot of smoke in the air in that direction. Paso Robles was burning.

This troubled Nod. He knew there were a few wineries and small towns where he might scavenge supplies soon. But he had had it in the back of his head that the larger stores in Paso Robles would be there when he needed them. Sure, he knew there had to be others still living in the area based on the math, but he really figured the whole 'societal unrest' aspect of the many post-apocalyptic scenarios he had studied wouldn't apply since the uninfected population would be so low. All that smoke made him worry a little bit more.

59

He stated thinking about his supplies. He was dangerously low on food. He had only one protein bar and one can of chili left and had been living a near-starvation reality already. He had enough water bottles for a few days, but it was getting hotter. For the first time, he started thinking seriously about leaving the rig.

They had passed quite a few wineries that had tasting rooms set-up along the highway for wine tours. Some were very elaborate while others looked more like Old West saloons. They had stopped at one on the way over and picked a bottle of wine that didn't survive the first night. The memory brought a smile to Nod's lips. Donna was an 'alley cat' when she had a few glasses in her. He had planned to stop on the way home and pick up more.

So, Nod sat and looked out at the horizon toward the coast. While the smarter bet for survival would be to head off toward the lesser-populated Central Valley, he decided he was going to stick around this area. As morbid as it sounded, he wanted the world to balance out again before he made any long-term decisions. As much as his life had changed in the past few days, he wondered with dread what the world would look like when the power goes out, medication dwindles, and food supplies go bad. Until that happened, he felt better being out here in the middle of nowhere.

***

Nod woke before the sun came up. It wasn't anything in particular that woke him, except maybe anxiousness. He began to pack his bag for the trip to the closest structure he could remember, a wine-tasting room near a vineyard, eight to ten miles west.

In his backpack he placed the last of his food, the protein bar, and two bottles of water. He'd leave the camp stove and most of his clothes for when he came back. He brought a change of underwear and some clean socks in case he was gone overnight. The binoculars and two grenades were tossed in as an afterthought. The last thing he added was Dorothy's blanket.

He added three full magazines for the rifle in the outside pockets. At first, he thought he would leave the rifle since it was so heavy. However, after some deep thought, he realized he could come across a pack of infected dogs, or people, and the pistol wasn't enough against multiple assailants. At least, not in his hands.

Putting his hat on, he started off down the road. The sun was just starting to come up behind him an hour later as he came up over the first rise in the road. Apparently, his objective was a little further than he thought because he could now see for miles and it wasn't in sight yet.

The walk was indeed longer than he realized with many hills and no cover from the sunlight. Though he had been an avid 'hiker' in Portland, his hikes consisted mostly of man-made paths around the city with lots of trees and flat asphalt-covered lanes for walking and biking. Very stroller friendly. Still, it surprised him how easily he covered the distance, with so many tall hills, on foot. The long trek didn't tire him out as much as he expected.

It was nearly three when he finally saw his objective. He had stopped under a tree and had just drained the last of his water when he took out his binoculars. The small building surrounded by tall oleanders loomed in the distance, only a few miles away. He almost shouted 'Yes!' but realized he might not be alone in the area.

He sped up as he neared. Half a dozen assorted vehicles were parked in the small, gravel-covered parking lot. Just outside the oleanders, he paused to look around. The building itself was a single story, possible an old house at one time. There were lots of windows, but they were covered in reflective film so he couldn't see inside.

His mind raced with all the possible scenarios. Did anyone live there or was it just a storefront? Strictly from a math point of view, there were more likely to be infected inside than normal humans. But the infected aren't quiet, so he was pretty sure it was empty of them, anyway.

Nod took his backpack off and placed it in the oleanders. He checked the pistol to see that the safety was off, then re-holstered it. That would be his backup. He then checked the rifle to be sure there was a fresh magazine and that it was ready to go. He walked over to the reflective glass doors, his rifle up to his chest.

With his left hand, he slowly pulled the door open. Inside, the lights were on and classical music played in the background. Cool, conditioned air hit him like a wall.

"Hello?" Nod called aloud, then repeated it louder. "Hello!"

There was no response. Nothing to indicate anything was alive. There was, however, a faint smell of decay. The entryway was small but opened on the left to a larger room with tables and a bar. There were pictures on the wall of vineyards and other scenic vistas. Behind the long wooden bar, there was a small commercial kitchen.

There were wine bottles covering all twelve tables as well as the bar. They were in various states of emptiness, but most hadn't been opened. At first, Nod thought maybe there had been a party, but then realized this was probably how it always looked. It was a tasting room, after all.

Though he was hungry, he decided to check the whole building before raiding the refrigerator. Luckily, the building wasn't very big. Beyond the kitchen, Nod found two doors.

The first door opened to a storeroom, filled with glasses, paper products and even some canned and dried food. Nod was surprised that there wasn't any wine in there. They must store it at the main winery somewhere close by, he figured.

The second door opened a small office. As soon as it cracked open, Nod knew he found the source of the smell. Lying on a very comfortable-looking leather couch was the body of an older man. He was covered in his own blood and had obviously been dead for days. Nod looked around the room to see if there was anything worth checking and, finding nothing obvious, he turned the light off and shut the door.

The refrigerator held an array of finger foods that Nod assumed went well with wine including many pounds of different cheeses and cured meats. An opened gallon and an unopened gallon of whole milk sat in the bottom. There was also a large container of spaghetti and meatballs that looked like someone's lunch. He stuck that in the microwave and turned it on.

While he waited for his 'spaghetti feast' he decided it would be smart to check the cars outside. Maybe there would be keys in one, so he didn't have to walk anymore. The timer on the microwave still had three minutes remaining as he walked back out the front doors.

There was a truck that looked like it was used for deliveries at one time. It was old, dusty, and looked like it hadn't moved in a while. Parked next to that was an old Volvo station wagon. It was clean, but obviously old. Nod knew almost nothing about car repair or maintenance, so he decided not to use that one either.

The other four cars included two newer minivans, a small truck, and an SUV. He checked the minivans first. Both were empty of anything useful and neither had their keys. The small truck had a decaying body sitting in the driver seat that had spewed blood all over the interior. Nod crossed that one off the list, too.

The SUV was the last in line. The driver-side door was open, and he crept up to it, the rifle up at his chest. Peeking inside, his heart sank. The bodies of an African American family were sitting inside. The 'mom and dad' were in the front, covered in blood, faces, frozen in the pain. The child, maybe eighteen months old, was strapped into a car seat in the back. Its face, he didn't know if it was a boy or girl, was much more serene.

Nod stumbled back and bumped into the oleanders. He fell to his knees and sobbed. He wept deeply. His anguish very vocal this time. And he wanted to hit something.

As his spasms of rage calmed, he heard a sound that brought him back to the moment. He wiped his eyes and raised the rifle as he stood up. He scanned the area looking and listening for anything. Slowly, he walked back over to the glass doors and turned to go inside.

The sound came again, and he brought the rifle up again. As he looked around, he saw movement under the SUV. He bent slightly as he approached and saw two cottontails hopping around underneath. He wondered if it was it the same two.

"Hello, Ladies," Nod greeted them with a smile. When he reached the SUV, he knelt on one knee and watched them hop around. They bolted into the oleanders.

Nod didn't chase after them this time. He knew he would see them again. He wondered, though, why they were here. Did they want him to use this vehicle? Then, he heard another sound. It was a weak moaning and it was coming from the SUV.

Nod's first thought was one of the parents must be infected. He came around the SUV and trained the rifle on them as he slowly advanced. But the sound came again, and it came from the back seat.

Dropping the rifle to hang by his side, Nod carefully slid the back door open. He half-climbed inside to get a closer look at the child. It hadn't been moving, but right then it's face contorted.

"Infected," Nod whispered. The thought of putting the baby out of its misery sent shudders through him, but he knew he couldn't walk away from it. He pulled his pistol and pointed it at the baby. As Nod began to apply pressure to the trigger, the tiny cherub's eyes opened slowly and glanced over at him. The contorted face softened, and a weak smile replaced it.

"Holy shit!" Nod screamed. "You're alive!"

CHAPTER 7

Nod's motions were a blur. He quickly and skillfully removed the child from the car seat and put an arm through the diaper bag sitting next to it. He rushed inside and lay the baby on the small couch in the entrance.

The child may have been in the car close to two days, at least. During the day, it had to be well over a hundred degrees in there. It should be dead. But it had a few lucky breaks, Nod determined. The driver's door had been left open and the passenger window was down. Also, the car was parked so that it was shaded by the oleanders during the hottest part of the day. Still, the baby had to be severely dehydrated.

Nod took off his backpack and unslung his rifle. He ran to the kitchen and found some clean hand towels that he soaked with cool tap water. He raced back to the child and put the cool towel on top of its head, then used the other to wipe it's face clean. The baby smiled weakly through cracked, chapped lips.

Nod fished a sippy cup out of the diaper bag and filled it with water and a couple of ice cubes. He swirled it around to make it as cold as possible as he hurried back. He used a cushion to prop the baby up, then put the short spout to its lips and turned it up slightly.

Its mouth moved as the cool liquid swirled inside. Nod was careful to let only a few drops in at a time, but within a minute, the baby was drinking greedily. A few times

Nod let too much flow and the baby gagged and hacked but resumed drinking as soon as it was able to draw a breath. This is how they spent the next half-hour, then the baby fell asleep.

Nod was not a doctor, but he decided to see if there was anything obviously wrong with the baby. He left it in a reclining position, for now, in case it threw up while it dozed. There was a clean onesie and diapers in the bag, so Nod stripped the baby down to inspect and clean it up.

"Well, you're a girl," Nod stated to her as he carefully removed the many-times-over soiled diaper. Unfortunately, he had to use most of the baby wipes in the bag to clean her up as poop had dried out in a ring around her backside. Soon she had a clean bottom, a fresh diaper, and an unsoiled onesie with pink roses on the front.

Nod found four small bottles of baby food in the bag and set them aside. He'd give her a jar later after he gave her some of the milk he had seen in the fridge. There was small jar of petroleum jelly, so he rubbed a little on her cracked lips. He found two more sippy cups and a bottle of teething gel. As he sat the bag down, he noticed a tag on the inside of the bag.

"This bag belongs to Elizabeth," he read. "Nice to meet you, Elizabeth. My name's Nod."

As the girl slept, he went outside to look through her car. There was luggage in the back as well as an assortment of baby travel items. Nod found a small swing, a jogging stroller, a travel playpen/bassinet, and a backpack carrier. There was a larger diaper bag that contained a full pack of diapers, two unopened packs of baby wipes, two large baby blankets, some talcum powder, and baby oil. Everything was packed neatly. "They were on vacation," Nod mumbled to himself. "Just like us."

He brought everything inside and placed it on the various tables. After reheating and devouring the spaghetti and meatballs from earlier, he sat up the playpen/bassinet in a corner of the room where there were no windows. Then he woke her to feed her some of the whole milk. When she finished, she burped loudly and went right back to sleep. This time, he put her in the bassinet and covered her with a baby blanket.

The sun was going down outside, so Nod shut all the blinds and made sure the doors were locked. He didn't want to draw any attention should there be anything or anyone roaming around outside. He couldn't block all the light coming from the building, so he used as few lights as he could.

He opened the mother's suitcase. It contained clothes, a couple of romance novels, and a toiletry bag. Nod removed what he could use and put everything else back inside. He sat the bag in a corner.

The husband's suitcase was a little more fruitful. He was nearly Nod's size, so Nod had some extra t-shirts and pants. The socks and underwear appeared to be clean. The toiletry bag even had a shaving kit and other necessities.

The biggest score in the husband's suitcase, though, was a very thin laptop computer with a large screen. Nod tapped the power button and prayed it wasn't password protected. And to his supreme joy, it wasn't.

Nod had been using his phone to access the internet and that worked alright. Unfortunately, Nod would soon have a problem with his vision. He wore contact lenses so he could see things up close, like his phone. The problem was he wore disposable contacts that were only meant to be worn for a month, then tossed. He knew from prior experience that you couldn't go too far beyond before the lenses began to irritate his eyes. He could clean them and get another few weeks, but there was no contact lens cleaner out here. He needed a bigger screen if he was going to surf the internet and now, he had it.

It took a few minutes to access the wi-fi in the building. He had to go back the office where the rapidly decaying body was found and find the router. Then he jotted down the default password printed on the label. He had written an article a few years back on resetting the wi-fi password to the default factory setting. He assumed they had changed it but went back to the laptop to type it in just to be sure. As he was typing, he noticed for the first time a sign on the wall that said, 'Free Wi-Fi for Customers' and below that was printed the password 'WeLoveWine'. Nod chuckled at his obliviousness and typed it in.

Nod typed in some of the websites he had been using to get updated information. None of the government websites had been updated in days. There was only one large news site functioning, Alpha News, and, according to them, there were only three employees still working out of thousands previously there. These three people were now living in the New York skyscraper that housed the main offices and had barricaded themselves inside to escape the infected roaming the streets. They spent their time now gathering as much global information as they could and dispensing it.

There were some social websites still updating, though most were offline. They were a chore to use, though, because you had to search for people still uploading and if they weren't your 'friend' already, it took time.

The best sources of information were the social media sites setup like old school bulletin boards. People posted whatever they want, gave it a hashtag, and then you simply looked for any new posts. Some had set up threads as the outbreak began and survivors were still posting to it.

One of the newest updates concerned Nod. Early reports had speculated that the infected would likely die off within a week of becoming symptomatic. The reason was simple: they would die of thirst. The human body needed water, and most cannot go more than three days without their kidneys shutting down followed by the rest of the body soon after.

The infected were driven by a constant adrenaline release and pure insanity. No one had ever been observed stopping to drink or eat anything. Even when they bit and tore at their victims, they eat any flesh.

Still, the infected weren't dying even a week later. One man, a prison guard in the England, wrote that prisoners in their cells had been infected for over three weeks. Some had died and others were slowing down significantly. But a small percentage were moving just as quickly and acting just as viciously as they had from the beginning.

"Like a true zombie," Nod mused out loud. "Great."

Nod's long-term plan, in the back of his mind, had been to hang out on the fringes of civilization until all the infected were dead. Then he would initiate contact with a group of survivors and help rebuild society. It wasn't anything he had really worked out, but more of a general idea. But now he needed to reassess things.

And, of course, there was Elizabeth now. He certainly couldn't take care of her. She needed a mom, not a 'mister mom'. While he had been Dorothy's primary caregiver, he wasn't the same as her mother. She was a better nurturer by far. He could feed her and change her and take her to day care and appointments, but Donna was always 'the mom.' She knew girls because she was a girl. And Elizabeth was African American. She might have skin and hair requirements he wasn't aware of.

So, he decided as he closed the internet browser that he would find Elizabeth a home. Or, at the very least, a mother. She needed someone that could do the things he couldn't.

As he sat in thought, his eyes caught sight of the beautiful background picture of the family. He then realized why the parents had both died from the infection and Elizabeth had survived. The picture showed them holding a mock Certificate of Adoption with all their names written on it.

Nod found the original photo and clicked on its information tag to see if there was a date. Sadly, it was dated only a month ago, when her dad likely downloaded it to the laptop. So, Nod knew only that she was adopted by Jonathan and Judith Hayes and it was more than a year ago, based on how young Elizabeth looked in the picture. She wasn't biologically related to them.

Nod closed the laptop and walked around the room, stretching. He quietly moved a comfortable chair near the bassinet, then found a tall floor lamp and put it there, too. He had another sippy cup of milk in the fridge ready for an early morning feeding if Elizabeth woke.

Nod turned off all the lights except for the floor lamp. The half-full moon shined its light through the secured double glass doors at the side of the large tasting room. He took Dorothy's blanket out of his backpack and covered his legs. He had turned the air conditioner down, so it wasn't cold, but he felt better with it on.

He turned to look at Elizabeth and put a hand on her stomach. He felt her steady heartbeat and the rise and fall of her breathing. He had done this a thousand times with

Dorothy when she was a baby. He then reached over and turned off the lamp.

"Good night, Elizabeth," he whispered and pulled the blanket up to his chin and closed his eyes. "Good night, ladies."

CHAPTER 8

Nod awakened to movement in the room. Shaking the sleep from his mind, he scanned the room and saw Elizabeth sitting up in her bassinet, smiling and looking at him. She was a little big for the bassinette, but it appeared comfortable enough.

"Well, good morning, Elizabeth," Nod stated with a yawn. He then stood and stretched.

The girl's smile broadened. She leaned forward in an obvious 'pick me up' move. Nod smiled and pulled the girl up into his arms. They walked over to a large window and Nod opened the blinds.

The two peered out at the bright morning. The window looked south, toward the many acres of grapes. The long lines of vines ran up the side of the hill and disappeared to the other. Nod figured the main vineyard area, with areas for processing and bottling and probably a large shop area for vehicles, must be on the other side of the hill, but he wasn't sure. The online map of that area hadn't been updated in years and only this building appeared on it. The rest showed open scrub land.

"How about a change and some breakfast?" Nod asked her rhetorically. Elizabeth chirped and jumped in reply.

After a quick diaper change, Nod fed Elizabeth a jar of pureed butternut squash. She seemed to enjoy it, but the more Nod thought about it, he remembered giving Dorothy mostly adult food by the time she was her size. They would

75

just cut it small. Still, the jars were packed by her mother, so she must have still been supplementing. He gave her a cup of milk when she finished the jar and sat her in the playpen.

Nod ate the last of the spaghetti and meatballs, the best he had ever tasted, then he attacked his list of chores for that day. The first thing he wanted to do was inventory their food. Next would be to surf the internet to determine where he should look for Elizabeth's new home. Third would be a sink bath for him. Finally, he wanted to figure out a suitable nickname for Elizabeth.

The pantry had a lot of stuff on its metal wire shelves. There were two, five-gallon bottles of water for a water cooler that Nod couldn't find. So, that gave him ten gallons of water if it stopped flowing from the tap. The only other bulk item was three gigantic cans of chili beans. Great for him, but not something he would give Elizabeth.

There was a lot of dried pasta in various configurations that Nod couldn't name. Luckily, there many cans of tomato sauce and tomato paste to go with the pasta. Rounding out the canned food was a dozen cans of fruit, vegetables and six small cans of Vienna sausages.

In the refrigerator was a gallon and a half of whole milk that expired in a few days. Nod figured it could go a bit beyond that date if it still smelled okay. There were six huge blocks of different cheeses, that were unfortunately not labeled, three large sticks of pepperoni, three large sticks of salami, a big box of crackers, a large jar of fancy mustard, and three long loaves of some kind of small, hard bread.

Nod decided to search the cabinets while he was at it and he was glad he did. He found an unopened bag of dried milk and a huge sealed can of dehydrated eggs. The rest of the cabinets included wine glasses and various serving hardware.

There was a large chalkboard in the entryway he brought into the kitchen. He listed all the things they had and estimated how many meals from each. He figured the best case scenario was, if they ate three times a day, with him mostly eating a snack for lunch, they had two full weeks of food. That assumed the tap water held out and the electricity kept the refrigerator going. If he cut his meals in half, they might stretch it to three weeks, but he wouldn't be in great shape to travel after that.

Just then a large pounding sound came from the tasting room. Nod ran around the bar to Elizabeth. As he passed the window, they had been looking out earlier, he saw an angry, haggard man slamming his arms against it. He was infected from the snarl on his face, but he wasn't moving fast or slamming his fists very hard. *This one was losing steam,* Nod thought.

Nod stopped and considered the situation. The window was thick, with at least two panes, and the man was weak. He probably couldn't break it easily but if he kept going, he might weaken it. He couldn't shoot the man through the window or the window would break, obviously. So, he decided he would go outside and shoot him and hope nothing happened to him for Elizabeth's sake.

He picked up the rifle and checked to make sure it was loaded. Then he flipped the safety off and set it to fire a single round at a time. His pistol was in its holster on his right hip if he needed it. He wished he could put Elizabeth in the office for safety, but the rotting corpse in there wasn't safe at all. The infected man was standing not far from the locked side door, so Nod couldn't use that one. Unfortunately, he had no way of locking the glass double doors from outside since he didn't have a key, but it would have to do.

He crept out the front doors and came around the front of the building where the parking lot was. He could hear the man hitting the window, but each blow was weaker than the last. Nod scanned the area to look for any other visitors and found none.

He brought the rifle up to his chest and turned the corner. As the barrel tipped out, the infected man slammed into Nod, both spilling on the ground. The rifle was knocked away from him since he hadn't secured the carrying strap. He quickly rolled away from the infected, who rolled more slowly.

Nod popped up on one knee and fumbled for the pistol in holster. He glanced down to see what the problem was, his heart pounding in his ears. He finally unsnapped the strap and pulled it free. He brought the pistol up, the barrel two feet from the chest of the advancing infected. Three shots rang out and the infected man fell forward toward Nod. The body glanced off him as he leaned to the side. He lay on the ground, unmoving, with a large puddle of blood collecting under him.

"Glad you were a stumbler and not a runner," Nod said to the dead man as he stood. Nod kicked the body, the pistol still trained on it, and it didn't move. The sound of breaking glass caused him to spin around.

Directly behind where the man had been shot, one of the windows of the building had a large hole in it. One or more of the bullets had passed through the man and hit the window. Another large chunk fell as Nod stared.

"Elizabeth!" Nod cried and ran toward the doors. He pulled them open and ran through. Coming around the corner, he saw her, sitting in her playpen, playing with a doll, and staring in the direction of the broken window. He ran over and picked her up, being careful not to frighten her.

"Hey, little girl," he whispered in a pleasant voice. "Did that noise scare you?" She hugged him, being playful. "I'm sorry, sweetie. I had to take care of that mean man." She let go and looked back at the playpen, so Nod put her back down.

He walked over to broken window, smacking his forehead. "Stupid, stupid, stupid," he whispered to himself. "Always look past what you're shooting at. *Call of Duty* 101." He examined the opening, then pulled out a few more chunks and tossed them outside. The blinds were stretched out a little, but undamaged.

"What am I gonna do about the window?" he asked himself, tapping his chin. He went over his mental checklist of resources and didn't remember any nails or screws or a hammer or drill. There were some plastic trays inside, but none were big enough on their own to plug the hole.

He went outside and walked around the building. There were several wooden pallets in the back that would be perfect for blocking the window, but he had no way to secure them. He dragged a couple of them around the front with him anyway.

As he stood at broken window, he thought about the truck. The back of it was tall enough to block the hole but not too tall that it wouldn't fit under the canvas awning. He looked over at it and saw two tires were low, but not flat. Still, there was no way he could push it.

He walked over to check out the truck more closely. The driver's door opened easily and didn't squeak. The interior was still clean but no keys anywhere to be found.

"The office!" he shouted. "They might be in the office."

Nod went back inside, waving to Elizabeth as he walked back to the office. He had stuffed a towel under the door and when he moved it, the smell of rot hit him hard. He put his shirt over his noise and went inside.

He quickly moved to the desk and searched for the keys. He held his breath if he could, but finally had to breath. It was disgusting. After searching every drawer and cabinet in the room, he found office supplies, receipts and other papers, a bottle of Absinthe, an old nudie magazine and no keys. Frustrated, he turned to the corpse on the couch.

"Where's your keys, man?" he asked angrily. As if hearing a reply, Nod responded to his own question. "Oh, yeah, probably in your pocket."

Reluctantly, Nod walked over to the couch. It looked comfortable, but the filth covering now made it forever unusable. The man was face down and Nod hoped and prayed the keys were in his exposed right pocket. But when he felt he pocket, it was empty.

"Lovely," Nod stated, trying not to breath.

He grabbed the man's belt and rolled the hips toward him. A jet of putrid air escaped from somewhere deep inside the corpse and Nod nearly threw up. He quickly dug his hand into the pocket and felt and large ring of keys. He pulled his reward out and let the body fall back. He then ran from the room, trying not to lose his spaghetti breakfast.

A few minutes later, Nod was sitting in the driver seat hitting his head on the steering wheel. It wasn't until now he realized the truck had a manual transmission. He had never driven a 'stick-shift' in his life. He knew you had to push the clutch in and do something with the stick, but that was it. He spent the next ten minutes online learning how to drive again.

It took him five tries to get the truck moving. He slowly let the clutch out and pressed the accelerator. The truck creeped along, but that was fine with Nod. He only had to move it twenty feet. He cranked the wheel and lined up the truck, so it almost grazed the building, then stopped when the truck box blocked the window. He got out to check the clearance and smiled at his precision parking. He was gonna 'cool off the neighborhood' with conditioned air that escaped, but nothing larger than a mouse could fit between the truck and the window.

Nod checked the key ring and found a large Volvo key. He was gratified that it was an automatic, and it started right up. It even had half a tank of gas. He shut it off and went back to the glass doors. After a couple of tries, he found the key that locked them, too.

He returned inside, locking the door behind him. Elizabeth was standing in the playpen, looking at him as he approached. "Well, Elizabeth, I inventoried our supplies, killed a man, broke a window, stole a dead man's keys, learned to drive a stick-shift, parked a panel truck with incredible precision and finally got a Volvo. Would you like some lunch?"

Elizabeth gave him a smiling raspberry as a reply.

"I'll take that as a 'yes'."

CHAPTER 9

The next ten days passed with very few problems. Nod had to kill one infected person, a woman this time. He was able to see her coming. She was faster than the last one, but Nod took her down in two shots before she was within a hundred feet.

Another infected German Shepherd had found its way to the building. It tried feverishly to claw its way through the side metal door. Nod shot it with only one round right through the door. Luckily, it left only a small round hole.

Elizabeth, whom they mutually decided would go by 'Lizzy' now, was walking around the tasting room a lot and getting her clothes dirtier as a result. Nod was learning to wash clothes in the sink well using dish soap. And setting them out to dry in the summer sun worked quickly. But their supplies overall were starting to run low and Nod knew he needed to do a little scouting. And he couldn't leave Lizzy by herself.

Unfortunately, Lizzy's car seat was in terrible shape after she sat in it for so long. The smell of her refuse as well as the odor from her decaying parents wouldn't come out no matter how much he washed the cloth cover and straps. So, he decided that she would be belted in the back seat with blankets and clothes rolled up around her and he would drive slowly and carefully.

He packed his backpack with a little food and some water bottles. The rest of the supplies were placed in the back of the wagon except for his rifle and three magazines, which lay on the seat next to him. This was just a scouting run, but he wanted to be ready in case they had to move on.

He had two destinations in mind. The first was the rig. He had left some of things there including clothes and ammunition because it was too heavy.

His second destination was a small store, and they had stopped at to get road goodies. It was about thirty miles east of the rig, closer to the valley. He picked it because it was, quite literally, in the middle of nowhere. There were very few homes nearby and the closest town was over ten miles away. It was a tourist trap, boasting itself as the last place James Dean stopped before dying in a car accident just up the road.

It took only fifteen minutes to get to the rig even though he kept his speed low. Everything was just how he left it, only dustier. He loaded his remaining items into the back of the wagon, then took Lizzy to meet 'the ladies.'

Lizzy sat in his arms as they stood by the mounds of dirt. Almost as if she knew it was a solemn, moment, she held his arms tightly and leaned her head on his neck as she looked down.

"Hi ladies," Nod started. "I know we talk a lot and if you can see us, you already know about my friend here. But I wanted you to officially meet Miss Elizabeth Hayes. She lost her parents, so I've been looking out for her the last few weeks. She's a good kid." Nod paused. "Please don't think

I'm replacing you, honey. She was just in a tight spot and needed help. As soon as I find her a new mommy, I'll be back on my own, as it should be."

After saying goodbye, they returned to the wagon. Lizzy settled into the back seat looking tired already. Nod started on, again not breaking fifty as he drove. He drove for ten minutes before he spotted something in the road. Light glinted off it as he pulled up next to a small, flat box.

Nod opened the car door and looked down at a cell phone. He picked it up and studied it. The screen was cracked, and it was dead, but he was sure it belonged to Al. The Dodger emblem on the back matched the one he had seen him carrying. He tossed it into the floorboard, saving its contents for something, someday.

The drive took longer than he remembered. He passed two burned out wrecks along the way. One involved a large farm truck leaving the road and flipping a few times. No one could have survived it, Nod told himself. The second involved two small cars. It appeared one tried to pass the other and didn't quite get all the way around. The two car bodies were entangled loosely. No one alive there, either.

It was hot outside. The closer they got to the valley, the hotter it got. They traveled past a few orchards, maybe almond or pistachio, Nod didn't know the difference. But they looked dry. He assumed the irrigation must be done manually instead of being automatic like his lawn. Given the extremely high temperature and low chances for rain, he reckoned the orchards were probably not going to make it to harvest in the fall.

He finally saw the market in the distance when they were a mile away. It was large to hold the many tourist goodies it held, but air temperature that was already nearing one hundred degrees before noon, made the air hazy.

Nod pulled off the road and took out his binoculars. He scanned the area for anything dangerous then got out. He focused the binoculars on the market for several minutes but didn't see any movement. He decided to move in closer.

Despite the ruralness of the area, there were a row of old houses about a mile south. It looked like maybe a dozen or so total. If anyone were still alive there, survivor, or infected, they would likely be attracted during the night to the brightly lit market.

He pulled slowly into the parking lot. There were a dozen vehicles, some parked correctly, others more willy-nilly. He circled the market several times, looking for any kind of movement. He saw none.

Nod pulled the wagon underneath the gas pumps where a large roofed structure provided some shade. He glanced back at Lizzy, and she was sound asleep. He debated leaving the wagon running so the AC would keep it cool for her but decided just to roll the front windows down a little and shut it off, leaving the keys in the ignition. He grabbed the rifle and headed toward the market.

His eyes flittered back and forth from the market to the cars parked nearby. He kept the rifle up at his chest, the safety off and finger off the trigger. It was only thirty feet to the door, but it felt a lot further.

The automatic doors opened as he got close. The cool air enveloped him like a cloud as did the smell of decaying flesh. Most of the cars had dead people inside, but some must have made it into the market before dying.

Nod walked around the large open building, searching down each short aisle, for anything that moved. He found three bodies sitting next to a picnic table. A few minutes later, he found two more in the large, walk-in freezer. It didn't look like any of them had been moved, they just died where they were sitting. Nod figured the two in the freezer might have been trying to survive longer in the cold air.

Nod grabbed a cold energy drink from the refrigerator. He opened and chugged half it in one gulp. His eyes teared up and he let out a burp as he wiped them.

"Ah, that's good!" he yelled.

The space in the wagon was limited, so he had to choose his supplies wisely. He found cardboard boxes and filled them with canned foods. There was also a lot of dried pasta. Everything he could find that was canned, bottled, or dried was potentially on the menu. Luckily, this store had a large assortment of freeze-dried fruits and nuts for the tourists. After three trips with a small flatbed cart, the wagon was full.

Nod's last load included some fresh vegetables and fruits that had not gone bad yet. He put that box in the passenger floorboard. The wagon was loaded down.

He went back inside and took one last look around. It dawned on him that he was at a gas station and the wagon needed gas. He looked at which pump he sat closest to, then went to the register where the pump controller was. Luckily. Nod had worked at a gas station when he was in college and knew what to do. After pushing a few buttons, pump #3 was ready for a fill up.

Nod debated whether to turn the lights off when he left. A lit building would certainly draw the infected. However, it would also draw survivors that needed supplies and there was plenty left inside. He might never be back this way again and anyone who needed it should be able to get to it. He did do one thing, though. He turned the automatic door off by flipping the power switch that operated it. You could still push it open or closed by hand, but this would help keep the wild animals out. He pushed the doors closed behind him.

The third pump was close enough to the tank cap that he didn't need to move the wagon. He took the cap off and grabbed the gas pump nozzle. Right away he noticed something was off and put the nozzle back on the cradle. The opening to the tank looked much bigger than normal. Suspecting he knew the answer, Nod looked at the side of the wagon where the model number was printed.

"Ah, it's a diesel," he mumbled. He looked around and found that eighth pump had diesel. He drove the over to pump eighth pump and parked. Before opening the door, he turned to Lizzy, whose eyes were now opened.

"I have to run back inside for a second, Lizzy. I started the wrong pump." He chuckled at himself while Lizzy didn't respond.

Nod opened the door and stepped out. Almost immediately he heard a low growl and feet sliding on concrete. He pulled the pistol from its holster and scanned the area.

The attack came from under the wagon. Teeth sunk into his right calf and push his leg out in front him. He tumbled backward from the sudden attack. It was not a large dog, but it was strong. It ripped at his calf muscle and Nod screamed.

He tried to aim the pistol, then quickly realized it wasn't in his hand. He kicked hard at the dog with his heel. Its muzzle was clamped down tight and barely flinched as the kicks connected. Nod looked around frantically for the pistol and spotted it just underneath the car. He reached for it as the dog pulled him further away, causing Nod to scream.

He continued to kick at the dog's face, now bloodied from Nod's shredded calf and its own splintered nose. Three more stiff kick caused the dog to release for a split second. That was all Nod needed to roll over to the pistol and grab it with his left hand. He then switched it to his right hand. The dog clamped down on the calf again, this time shaking it as it bit.

Nod howled and fired. The bullet missed and hit the ground near the front tire. The dog ignored it and continued to thrash. Nod fired three times fast, hoping to strike it through his blurring vision. The dog let go.

Nod's eyes cleared long enough to see the dog still moving. He fired twice more, hitting the dog both times. It stopped moving.

Nod wiped his eyes and sat up. He could see the mangled flesh under his pant leg, and his right shoe looked shredded, too. He didn't even remember the dog biting him there, but it happened so fast, he wasn't sure of anything. Blood poured out of him.

He heard a noise from the road and leaned over to see what it was. Half a mile away, an infected man was approaching. He was yelling unintelligibly and moving faster than he should be able to. He must have been at the houses Nod saw earlier and the gunshots drew his attention.

Nod struggled to rise at , but his adrenaline and fear eventually allowed him to ignore the pain in his right leg and foot. He steadied himself on his left leg and opened the door. He fell into the driver seat and started the car. He quickly checked on Lizzy, who seemed unimpressed by the whole ordeal, and put the wagon in drive.

Then nothing. Nod's damaged leg and foot wouldn't do as he asked. He used his left foot to hit the gas pedal and

90

he sped out of the parking lot, the infected man nearly at his bumper. It was several miles down the road before Nod didn't see him in his rearview mirror.

After another few miles, Nod pulled over. He had to stop the blood flowing out of his calf or else he would bleed to death. But he didn't have a lot of time. He pulled his T-shirt off and wrapped it tightly around his calf. He used his left shoe to push off his right shoe. Pain shot up his body and he clenched his teeth to keep from screaming. His sock was torn open, and Nod could see his third and fourth toe were gone. It wasn't bleeding a lot, but he still needed to wrap it. He grabbed another t-shirt, one he had just gotten from the market, and wrapped his foot.

He pulled back out onto the road, using his left foot to get the car back up to speed. Once he reached fifty, he put the cruise control on. His mind raced as he tried to figure out his next move.

"Get back to the tasting room," he recited to himself. "Clean and wrap the leg and toes. Take something for pain. Try not to die." He turned to the back seat. "That sound good, Lizzy?"

Nod had to slow and use his left foot again to go around Al's rig. Then he quickly sped up again. A few minutes later, the tasting room was in sight. As he turned into the parking lot, his hands were shaking. He looked down at his right leg and the blood was pooling in the floorboard. Lots of blood.

He turned to look at Lizzy. "We got a problem here, Lizzy. I've lost a lot of blood. If I don't get it to stop, I'll bleed to death and you'll be stuck alone in the tasting room. If I do get it to stop, I'm gonna pass out eventually and might not wake up for a long time, if at all. Again, you're alone. I'm afraid we need to find someone to take care of you now," Lizzy replied sadly.

Nod turned onto the small side road that ran by the tasting room. He knew there was a little town not too far away. Lots of rural houses. With luck, he could find someone still alive that could take in Lizzy. They could have all the supplies he had if they took her in.

Nod felt faint. His eyes blurred and were unfocused. He kept scanning the surrounding area, hoping to find some sign of life. His left leg cramped from using it to press the gas pedal.

Finally, he saw a house, maybe a mile off the road on the side of a hill. There were clothes on a clothesline. He spotted a dirt road but couldn't tell if it went to the house because of the number of trees. He slapped himself to stay conscious, so he took the chance and turned onto the road. He was almost out of time.

"I bet they have other kids, Lizzy," he stated wearily. He was doing everything he could to stay awake, but the blood loss was catching up. "Maybe they have a pool. Man, …I…would…have loved…. a pool….when I was…...a kid…." Nod's voice trailed off as he began to lose consciousness. He was vaguely aware of the wagon coming to an abrupt stop. "I'm…. so… sorry…. Lizzy…."

CHAPTER 10

Nod awakened. It was the second time in a month he was surprised to be alive. He tried to move and felt the ache of sedentary stiffness. He sat up slowly, he scanned the area. He was lying in a bed in a small room decorated in typical farmhouse fashion. There was a window covered in a blue, sheer curtain. Maybe it was a drape. He wasn't really sure what the difference was. All he knew was that it was light outside.

"Lizzy!" he blurted out, her face came to his mind. He tried to get out of bed and froze from the pain. He pulled the covers back to reveal his legs. His right calf was bandaged as were the toes of his right foot.

Then it came back to him all at once. The fight with the dog. The bites. The fast driving. Crashing? What had happened? How did he get here? Where was 'here'?

"We thought we heard movement," came a female voice from the door. Nod looked over to see a woman standing in the door, holding Lizzy. She was tall and slight. Her metallic gray hair was short, and she wore thick-rimmed glasses. If not for her tone of voice and the gentle curviness of her outline, Nod would have thought she was a guy.

"Lizzy!" Nod bellowed. "Is she okay?"

"She's fine," the lady replied. "And so are you, by the way." She brought Lizzy over and sat her on the bed next to him. She hugged him tightly and he returned it. The lady stuck out her hand.

"I'm Vivian Lake," she stated.

"Nod," he replied.

"Why? Am I agreeing to something?"

"No, my name's Nod."

"Just Nod?"

"Just Nod. And this is Elizabeth Hayes, Lizzy, who you've apparently already met. How did we end up here?"

"Your car hit one of my trees. Tripod, that's my dog, heard you coming up the road and started barking. You almost made it to the house, but we found your car sitting against a tree a little way up the road. It didn't do much damage to either one. You must have passed out, and the car just rolled. I pulled Lizzy out and brought her to the house first. Then I got a wheelbarrow and came back and got you. I sewed you up and gave you some antibiotics. You're healing fast, so you'll be fine soon. What happened?"

"An infected dog really did a number on my leg. I figured I'd never walk right again."

"Well, it did chew your calf up pretty good, but those toes were shot off, not bitten. I think you shot yourself trying to kill the dog," Vivian pointed out.

"Ugh, that sounds like something I would do," Nod replied, shaking his head in frustration.

"You only lost two and, like I said, you're healing fast. Really fast, to be honest."

"I guess I'll be okay as long as I don't need to count higher than eighteen," Nod mused. They both laughed and Lizzy joined in.

Vivian looked at Nod, then at Lizzy. "I don't mean to pry but she's not...?" Vivian began to say but stopped.

Nod chuckled. "No, she's not my daughter. I found her…. it's a long story."

"Well, we've got nothin' but time," Vivian replied. "I tell you what, let me grab some crutches next door, and we'll get you moved to the porch. You've been cooped up in here for two days."

"Two days?" Nod asked. "I've been asleep for two days?"

"Three actually, but the first day I kept you in the barn." Vivian gave him a wink. "Can't be too careful."

"Is that why I'm naked?" Nod asked, again with a chuckle.

"No, that was to keep things sterile. You were pretty dirty," Vivian yelled from the hallway. She returned a few seconds later. "Oh, don't worry about me seeing your penis. I've seen thousands of 'em. Most were way bigger than yours, though."

***

Vivian was a veterinarian who specialized in horses and cattle. Nod found that out after sharing some of his story with her. So, he wasn't too offended by her quip after she explained. The barn contained a well-equipped surgical room, which is where he had stayed originally.

As they sat on the screened-in back porch overlooking the property, she went on to talk about her background. She and her partner, Sam, were both vets and had been together for over thirty years. Sam coming late from a house call when he was killed by a drunk driver three years ago. They never had kids. They couldn't even adopt, according to Vivian, because of the stigma around their relationship back then.

Nod had a feeling Vivian was a lesbian but didn't care. Where he grew up in Portland, it was very progressive and not shocking at all. He knew her experience must have been a lot different in this area.

"You two must have had a tough time back then," Nod insisted.

"Most people didn't even realize it, so it wasn't a big problem. But government paperwork tells a different story. A more intrusive story," Vivian lamented.

"I had a cousin who had a similar problem," Nod sympathized. "Her wife looked like a male, lived her life as a male, but that didn't matter when they wanted to get married. They had to go to Hawaii to do it."

"Well, it's not quite the same thing. Sam wasn't a woman, he was black. Fairly light-skinned, but he couldn't lie to the government."

Nod was surprised. "I'm sorry, I just assumed…"

"That I was gay? Because I dress like a dude?"

"Uh, yeah."

Now Vivian chuckled. "No, I'm straight. It's just a lot easier to find good work clothes in the men's department. And messing with long hair got old after a few years of working on the ass-end of horses. You only have to wash horse shit out of your hair a few times before you cut it all off. And Sam didn't care, so I kept it that way."

They were both silent for a few minutes. Then Nod said, "It's so beautiful here. There's more trees than where I was before. Greener in general."

"The closer you get to the coast, the more moisture there is in the air."

"Have you had any trouble? From the infected?" Nod asked.

"A few infected people. A lot of infected dogs. There's a bunch of breeders around here. Infected dogs must have gotten out. I put them down. Why, you thinkin' of stayin' a while?"

Nod glanced down at Lizzy. She sat on a blanket that covered the green outdoor carpet of the porch. Vivian's dog, named 'Tripod' due to it missing one of its front legs, jumped around her. It was a large dog but a mutt. Nod couldn't even guess at the breeds.

"Well, I'm trying to find Lizzy something permanent. You seem like a caring person, resourceful even. If you could take care of her...?"

"Nod, Nod, Nod. I'm a sixty-five-year-old woman, and I've had some heart issues lately. Nothing serious, but enough to be of concern. I'd be a decent grandmother, but I'm too old to be a real mother to her. Why can't you both stay?"

"I can't really explain it. I'm a big fan of Lizzy. I'd die or kill for her, but I'm not a mommy. And I was already a daddy and it didn't work out. I was weak, I didn't prepare, and I lost everything. Maybe it would be wrong to have another child, like I was replacing Dorothy or something. It's complicated, at least in my head, you know?"

"Well, talk about washing horse shit out of your hair," Vivian stated. "You really think you can replace Dorothy? Or Donna, for that matter? They are with you forever, buddy-boy. You might go on to have twenty kids and not one of them would replace the one you lost. That's not how it works. She's a part of you, no matter what. I bet Lizzy is, too. It's just like if you and Donna had another kid. The second won't replace the first. You're just scared, Nod. Scared that what happened to your girls will happen to Lizzy."

"Don't beat around the bush, Vivian," Nod said sarcastically. "Tell me how you really feel."

"It's simple human nature, Nod. Fear drives us all."

They were quiet for a few minutes. Nod was processing his thoughts when Vivian chimed in.

"Look, stay here for a few days. Let your leg heal and maybe you can help with some chores when you're able. There's room for both of you here if you want to stay permanently."

Nod shook his head in the affirmative. He needed to think about what to do with a future he never expected to have.

***

Three days later, Vivian was changing the dressing on Nod's leg. She inspected his calf and foot thoroughly, a frown on her face the whole time. She set his foot down on the ground gently.

"Looks good, right?" Nod asked. "It hasn't hurt in a while."

"Good is an understatement," Vivian replied. "Nod, the scars are puckered and pink. It's almost completely healed. Even your foot. It looks like the two toes were never there. This should have taken a month to heal to this degree. I don't get it."

"There were some people on the internet that said something similar had happened to them. Small cuts that had healed overnight. One guy said he had migraines every other day before the outbreak but hadn't had one since. Do you think it's the virus?"

"Maybe. I did notice when I loaded you into the wheelbarrow and then onto the exam table that it wasn't as hard as I expected. I just thought you weren't very heavy." Vivian thought for a moment. "Could be this virus is preserving us, like some of the infected. The ones that are still running around despite eating or drinking. Maybe it's rewriting our genetic code or just hijacking our immune system. There's no way I can tell with the equipment I have. But there is something I can do."

Vivian grabbed a clean scalpel. She rolled up her arm and cut a two-inch line up the middle of her forearm. It wasn't too deep, but the blood flowed out immediately.

"What are you doing?" Nod asked incredulously. He quickly reached out to stop her. She waved him off.

"I cut my arm just like this last year accidentally. It took a month to heal to a scar. And it was still tender for a while after that." She began to wrap it in gauze, then secured it with tape. "Let's see how long it takes this time."

"You're crazy, Vivian."

"You should have already figured that out, Nod."

***

It took two days. As they both examined the pink scar on Vivian's forearm, they marveled at its lack of blood or tenderness.

"And it doesn't hurt at all?" Nod asked.

"It hasn't since the first day," Vivian replied. "I think when you look at this and your internet research, it's undeniable. The virus is changing us."

"Into what? That's the question," Nod stated.

"Well, so far it seems we're a little stronger, maybe a little faster. Neither of us is taller nor shorter, no real change in weight. Certainly, we heal faster but with exception. Your toes aren't growing back. The infected woman you shot yesterday isn't healing. I checked the body this morning where we hog-tied it out back. If anything, she's decaying more quickly than normal."

"We're still getting hungry and thirsty, unlike some of the infected. And Lizzy isn't growing unnaturally, although I wonder if the virus is what allowed her to survive in the hot car for two days. Maybe the virus is just making us tougher?"

"Time will tell, Nod. Hopefully, that's all that happens."

CHAPTER 11

Three months later

"Say your prayers, Nod," the woman suggested.

"Every night with Lizzy, Sadie," Nod replied.

"Well, when you eat with the Millers, you say your prayers first. Give thanks," Sadie instructed.

Nod relented and bowed his head. The three, Nod, Sadie and Sadie's oldest son Dean, sat silently for a minute, then began eating their sandwiches. The cab of the Humvee was cramped, but they were used to eating there now.

"How many runs does this make for us?" Nod asked.

"The three of us?" Dean thought. "This'll be run number eight. For mom and me, ten."

"Seems like this is what we've always done," Sadie chimed in. "Four months since the world ended and it seems like a lifetime ago."

Sadie Miller was a client of Vivian. She and her family owned a horse ranch a few miles south of Vivian's place. She had lost Steve, her husband of twenty-odd years, to cancer two years before the virus broke out. Her son Dean was twenty-two and married. In an extreme stroke of luck, his wife, Millie, was also a survivor. His teenaged brother, Tex, often chided him, saying they must be related.

Unfortunately, the family lost most of their horses and livestock with the virus. Though they were well-stocked with their homemade canned food, they began doing small runs into surrounding towns to build up their supplies. When Vivian contacted them two months ago, Nod s joined them.

The Humvee they were currently eating in was one of four the two families had acquired. There was a glut of them along Highway 101 after the virus took out several military motorcades. The bonus was that they were easy to wash out with a hose. Two other families in the area they knew of also had Humvees.

"Well, we've never scored like this," Dean stated, pointing his thumb outside. "That tank has thousands of gallons of diesel."

"And you're sure you can drive it?" Nod asked.

"No problem," Dean assured him. "I drove a truck like that one halfway across Iraq. It runs well and the brakes aren't seized up. We'll park it behind our barn and use it as a filling station. I just need some pipes and fittings from the hardware store. Man, it'll be nice not having to siphon diesel out of the ground at the gas station. Gasoline is bad enough, but that diesel smell is nasty."

"We could snag a handle from one of the gas stations," Sadie suggested.

"I think they have some at that big hardware store," Nod said. "I remember seeing them when we got that fencing last month."

"You remember it because that was next door to that giant hobby shop with all the drones," Dean stated matter-of-factly. "I like to never have got you out of there."

Nod smiled. "There were dozens of them. Flyers, drivers, rocket propelled, you name it. I was in Heaven."

"Ah, boys and their toys," Sadie replied shaking her head. "So, we can get everything we need at the same place. We just need to get home with the diesel tank and the other stuff we found without drawing any attention."

"We haven't seen any Crazies in a few weeks," Dean noted. "And Stumblers aren't around much anymore."

"Bob Floss said they ran into a bunch of Crazies when they tried to get to San Luis Obispo two weeks ago," Nod reported. "At least five of them, working together."

"He told us that, too," Sadie responded. "Damn Crazies used to tear each other apart on sight and now they're banding together. Bob said they would have overrun his group for sure if it had happened at night, when they couldn't see them coming."

"I used to love San Luis," Dean lamented, shaking his head. "Best barbeque around."

"Best barbeque outside of your mom's grill, you mean," Nod corrected him.

Sadie blushed. "Aw, the flames do all the work."

Nod worried for a moment. Sadie's blushing came off as a reaction to him being flirtatious. He wasn't trying to be flirtatious at all. Sadie was very pretty, and Nod could hardly believe she was ten years his senior, but he didn't feel romantically toward her. That part of him died when he lost his family. Besides, he had lost Donna only four months ago. It was way too early for him to be thinking about that sort of thing.

"She is the best grill master of all time, but she doesn't carry the widest selection of beers that complement her handiwork," Dean noted. "We're down to *Pabst Blue Ribbon* and that doesn't complement anything."

"I practically lived on *PBR* during my college years," Nod stated. "It was cheap and did the trick." The three laughed together.

"Well, we should probably get this load home," Sadie announced, folding the plastic bag that held her sandwich. "It won't be easy to get that rig down the road. We'll probably have to use the Humvee to push some of the cars out of the way."

What would normally be a ten-minute trip took two hours. Nod drove the Humvee while Sadie navigated. He had to push thirty-five cars out of the way to get the rig off the highway and onto a side road that would get them to the Miller's ranch. It was easier to take the winding side roads three times the distance than try and fit the rig on the loaded highway.

Nod was getting to know these back roads better and better. Seeing anyone else was extremely rare, but they had run into a few people traveling to get to their loved ones, who were hopefully still alive. When they did, they offered whatever food and water they had with them, which was usually accepted.

They put down any infected they came across. Sometimes, they would be in a car or a business, secured from the outside, but the group would always put them down regardless of the immediate danger. Having any infected alive nearby just seemed like a 'loose end' that needed to be tied.

When they reached the Miller's ranch, they parked the rig carefully behind the barn. Then the two men unhooked the rig from the tank and parked it in the old pasture with the odd assortment of vehicles they had collected.

While Vivian's ranch had some open area for pastures, the Miller's ranch had hundreds of acres they used for pastures and training their horses. Just before the outbreak, they had almost fifty horses they trained or boarded and over a hundred head of cattle. Now, they had five horses, eight cows, and two bulls.

One of the large pastures was were all the vehicles were kept. There was construction equipment, flatbed trailers, tractors, farm implements, a forklift, and other machinery. Dean had brought in a short school bus and welded plate steel to it just in case they needed an armored vehicle. Several newer work trucks were lined up, including one with a bucket for working in the air. And at the back of the pasture were dozens of solar panels stacked on top of pallets.

The men returned to the house where Sadie had parked the Humvee. She sorted the supplies they had picked up into plastic boxes. Nod saw the toys he had found for Lizzy were already in his box.

"You're going to spoil that girl," Sadie mused. "She gets new toys every time you go out. What are you going to do for Christmas?"

"Depends," Nod replied. "You think she's a Corvette girl or a BMW girl?"

They all laughed, including Tex and Millie, who had come out to help them sort. When they were finished, Nod had three full boxes of food and toiletries and, of course, Lizzy's toys. Nod placed the three boxes back into the storage area of the Humvee.

"I'll drive you home," Dean told Nod. Sadie looked surprised as she normally drove Nod home but didn't say anything.

"Sounds good," Nod replied.

Though the two ranches were only a few miles away, the drive usually took a while. No one drove fast anymore because it wasn't worth the risk. And it saved fuel. Nod had walked to the Miller's ranch earlier that day partly to save fuel and partly because it was a nice day.

"We're plannin' on makin' a run to Templeton in a couple of days," Dean explained as they drove.

"Really?" Nod asked. "Kinda high population, isn't it?"

"Yeah, but Mr. Floss said they drove through and not a single Crazy came after them. And that solar company has their warehouse not too far into town. Just off the freeway, but no big sign."

"Oh yeah, we talked about them. The batteries for our solar arrays."

"I think we should check sooner rather than later. I'm afraid someone is gonna come across 'em and take 'em. Cindy Abrams told mom they've seen some signs that there may be some other group millin' around the area."

"If they even have them," Nod interrupted. "Just because their website says they sell them doesn't mean they kept them in stock."

"Don't you think it's worth the risk?" Dean asked.

"I do. If we lose power again, it may not come back on. We need to be ready for that."

"And you're sure you can hook it all up?" Dean asked with a smile.

"I think so," Nod reassured him. "I've been doing a lot of research and I think we have almost everything we need except the batteries. Hell, the Flosses, and the Abrams already had grid-tied solar systems. They just need the batteries and charge controllers. WE still have to build our entire systems."

"Maybe we can trade some batteries with Bob Floss," Dean suggested. "He's got two teenaged granddaughters. Maybe we can use the batteries as a dowry for Tex." The two men laughed heartily.

"There's something else I want to talk to you about, Nod," Dean stated, seriously as they pulled up to Vivian's house.

"Shoot," Nod replied.

"It's weird to talk about this, but you and mom…"

Nod stiffened. "Hold on, partner, there's nothing going on…"

Dean put his hands up to stop him. "No, no, I know, I know. It's just that, I've seen her look at you, here and there, like she's studying you. Trying to make her mind up about something. I know it hasn't been that long since your wife passed away, but, well, I don't know. I just wanted to let you know that eventually she'll be…available."

The last word hung there for a while, then both men burst out laughing. "Oh my gosh," Dean gasped. "This is so awkward."

Nod wiped his eyes. "No, man, I get it." Nod paused and thought for a moment. "You're a good son, Dean, but I just don't think I'll ever be ready for that kind of thing. Sadie is an incredible woman and a good friend, but after what I've been through, I don't think I'll ever be romantically involved again. My brain just won't go there anymore. It's broken."

"Well, maybe your brain will fix itself at some point," Dean urged. "Time heals and all that. Lord knows there's not a lot of people around anymore. We all need to find comfort. I want mom to feel that comfort again someday."

"How about Bob Floss?" Nod suggested.

"He's seventy, Nod! How old do you think my mom is?" The two burst out laughing again.

Nod removed the three boxes and stacked them by the gate. The new fence that surrounded the house and barn was sturdy and they always kept the two gates locked. He waved to Dean as the truck disappeared down the dirt drive. As Nod unlocked the gate and opened it, Lizzy came running out of the front door followed closely by Vivian.

"Nod!" Lizzy exclaimed, stopping at the top of the stairs. She had been saying his name for a month and it brought a smile to his face every time.

"Good girl stopping at the top of the stairs," Nod cheered loudly. "I'll be right there." Nod set the three boxes inside the gate and locked it from the inside. Even with a mechanical post hole digger, it had taken him and Vivian a week to put the fence up. And, being that it was the first thing he had ever really built, he couldn't help but admire it every time he saw it.

"You need help?" Vivian asked.

"Nah, they aren't too heavy," Nod replied, picking all three boxes up at once. The virus had made him stronger, maybe twice as strong as he had been, but he was far from Superman. He carefully climbed the stairs holding the stacked boxes out so he could see the steps. The virus hadn't decreased his natural clumsiness one bit. When he reached the top, Vivian took the top two boxes from him.

"Wow, looks like you found a lot of good canned food," she observed.

"Yep," Nod replied. "Lots of veggies and fruits. Even a couple of canned hams. Most of it still has a couple of years on the expiration dates."

"Me, me," Lizzy chirped, her arms out.

"Are you happy to see me, Lizzy, or just the toys I bring you?" Nod asked, reaching into a box.

"Me, Nod, me," Lizzy squealed excitedly.

Nod produced two stuffed animals, and Lizzy grabbed them tightly. One was a bear while the other was either a dolphin or a skinny whale, Nod wasn't sure. Lizzy didn't care either way. She released her hold on the stuffed animals only long enough to hug Nod.

"Tan' goo," Lizzy yelled into Nod's ear. Her speech was coming along, Nod thought. She seemed to be right there with Dorothy at that age. Sadly, they could only guess what that age was. Determined to give her a birthday, Vivian had chosen March 1st as the day they would celebrate her 2nd birthday.

Lizzy ran back inside, and Nod and Vivian followed. They brought the boxes into the kitchen and sorted through them. A few cans went into the pantry while most went into the root cellar through the door in the floor of the pantry.

The root cellar was not part of the original house. Vivian's husband had hand-dug it under the house years ago when Vivian had lamented having no space to put her home canned food. The possibility of not getting any more homemade jam scared him enough to spend a month digging it out, putting up support beams and cementing the walls and floors. The entire room was filled with rows of metal shelving containing many months, maybe even a years, worth of food.

Lizzy ran into the kitchen. "Gammy, look!" she bubbled, holding up the two new stuffed animals.

"I know, dear, I saw them," Vivian replied with a smile. "Did you name them?"

"Dis one Pete," she said, holding up the bear. "Dis one...Paul," she continued, holding out the dolphin/whale. Of the several dozen stuffed animals Lizzy had, all were named either Pete or Paul. They didn't know why she chose those names.

"Those are lovely names, dear. Now, why don't you go introduce them to all your other animals while I finish dinner?"

"Okay," the girl replied, running out of the room.

"She's fast," Nod noted.

"All toddlers are, but, man, I think she beats any I've ever met," Vivian replied with a chuckle. "You hungry?"

"Starved. Just let me go stow my gear and I'll come help you finish."

"Sounds good."

Nod brought his rifle and small travel belt to his room. His 'travel belt', as he called it, was a strong webbed cotton belt with loops and pouches to hold gear like spare magazines, a good knife, a small medical kit, etc. It was heavy and required a pair of suspenders to help keep it up. He sat it next to his bed but kept his pistol with him in its holster. He tossed his hat on the bed.

Checking to make sure the door was closed, he reached into the closet and pulled out a duffel bag. He placed it on the bed and unzipped it. Inside, small cans of tuna and chicken and larger cans of vegetables were visible. Nod reached into his pocket and brought out a fistful of beef jerky. From inside his shirt, he withdrew six packages of ramen. All were placed in the duffel bag. He put it back into the closet.

Nod looked at the calendar on the wall. It was three weeks until Thanksgiving. He sat on the bed and thought for a moment. He'd been planning his 'escape' for weeks. The day after Thanksgiving, he planned to leave and return to the rig and then move north. By then, he would have enough food and supplies for months on the go. Just three more weeks.

CHAPTER 12

Two Days Later

Dean and Nod used a tire iron to pry open the metal door leading to the solar company's warehouse. It was conveniently attached to the main store but had no connecting door inside. They had spent ten minutes quietly breaking into the store and another ten minutes searching for a door connecting the two spaces. Now, they were back at square one.

"It's starting to budge," Dean spat through gritted teeth. The door popped open, and the tire iron slipped out of their grip and fell to the asphalt. The sound of the impact rang loudly, causing Sadie to nearly jump out of her spot in the gunner's seat.

"Whew! I'm glad my finger wasn't on the trigger," Sadie exclaimed, from behind the big gun. She twisted from side to side, scanning the area.

"I'm sure the sound of the truck and trailer pulling up was louder than that," Nod affirmed.

Both men brought their rifles up to their chests and slowly walked through the door. Inside, the sunshine poured into the room through skylights. And as far as the eye could see, there were pallets of solar panels covering the space.

"Wow," Dean stated. "That's a lot of panels." He bent and looked closer. "They're all 200 watts. Dozens of 'em. I guess we know where to find more if we need 'em."

"Any Powerwalls?" Nod asked. "The company SAID they sold 'em."

"I don't see any, but there's a lot of pallets." Something caught Dean's eye. "Wait, that pallet with the smaller boxes by you. See it?"

"Yeah, too small to be panels." Nod knelt closer and saw the word *Tesla*. "This is it. Holy cow, this is it!"

Dean came over quickly. "You're right. There's four pallets of eight. That's thirty-two Powerwall batteries. We only need, what, two or three per house?"

"Three would be more than enough, according to their website. We can take two pallets and still have enough to share."

"Definitely," Dean agreed. "But I wouldn't mind hiding some either, just in case we need more later."

"Agreed."

Next door to the solar company's warehouse was a bridal boutique. Dean used a forklift to bring a single pallet of batteries over to the door then he and Nod moved each battery into the store by hand. They stacked them in a back office, hoping that, in the 'zombie apocalypse', no one would need a bridal gown for some time. All of this was done under the watch eye of Sadie.

When they finished loading the two pallets, they were taking home onto the flatbed trailer they had brought, they decided to take a break and have some lunch. They sat in the Humvee and ate their sandwiches while Sadie and Dean recounted their many family escapades. Nod never shared anything about his family and they never pried. Only he even knew his real name. When they were finished, they cleaned up and started back to the Miller ranch.

Sadie drove as Dean took his turn in the turret. Nod sat in the passenger seat, watching the scenery pass by slowly. He thought about his plan to move on soon. He would miss the friends he made, but their friendship hurt him. He didn't think he deserved to have friends if his family couldn't. And this idea was cemented by him not seeing the rabbits since he had arrived. He figured if he made sure Lizzy was safe, he could move on and he'd see the rabbits again.

The route through town was cluttered with cars. They had managed to use the Humvee to push most of them out of the way. As they drove back the same way, there were a few tight spots, but the truck and trailer only received a few new scratches for the most part.

The cars thinned as they reached the outer neighborhoods of town. Nod's deep thoughts were interrupted by the sudden slam of a large object hitting his door. He jumped and turned to look. The object was a body belonging to a Crazy.

Sadie had been through this scenario enough times that her natural reaction was no longer to stop, but to speed up a little. She spotted the Crazy in the rearview mirror and expected Dean to take it out from the turret, instead of a large gunshot report, she heard Dean yell, "Contact! Multiple!"

Nod grabbed his rifle from the floorboard. "Where?" he screamed in reply, scanning the area.

"Everywhere!" came the shaky reply, followed by a succession of small explosions from the 50-caliber turret.

"I can't speed up here!" Sadie warned. "Too many cars!"

Nod continued to scan the area but didn't see anything. But then he did. Crazies were coming from every direction between the cars. At least a dozen, he estimated. Nod could see Dean's bullets smashing into cars and asphalt as the Crazies lived up to their name.

"Just keep moving," Nod urged. He rolled down the window and stuck the barrel of the rifle outside. He began to take aim and fire, the loud barrage of sound from the exploding rounds drowning out all other sound in the cab. Unfortunately, he wasn't having any more luck than Dean.

"They're too fast!" Dean and Nod yelled almost in unison. Finally, Dean hit two Crazies that had been slowed by a large van blocking their way. The heavy rounds tore through their bodies nearly cutting them in half. But there was no time to celebrate as the rest of the Crazies were now too close for Dean to hit with the big gun. He pulled out his pistol and fired.

Nod pulled back the rifle back inside as the Crazies got too close. He, too, took out his pistol. Its small size allowed him to twist and move easier and he put a round in a Crazies' head just as it reached him. The rest seemed to be trying to dodge their fire. Nod had never seen Crazies do this and he was sure the others hadn't seen it either.

Sadie turned a corner and smashed the accelerator to the floor. The road was completely open with no cars in sight. Eventually, the Crazies couldn't keep up and fell back. Nod thought they gave up a lot easier than they used to. Dean was still popping off rounds intermittently, but not hitting anything.

"Okay, that's a new one," Sadie stated with exasperation.

"So, they really are working together now," Nod added.

"Looks that way. That's definitely going to complicate things."

"Maybe you should take a roundabout way back to the ranch. Just in case they're following."

"Good idea. I know a couple of cleared side roads we can take," Sadie assured him.

The trip took twice as long thanks to Sadie's 'side road' route. Nod had asked Dean if he wanted to come down from the turret since they were out of danger, but he declined saying the cool air felt nice. Nod figured he wanted him to have more time with Sadie. They had mostly just talked about the changing weather.

They stopped at Vivian's ranch first to drop off some of the batteries. Dean and Nod unloaded six and stacked them in the barn. Nod surveyed the stacks of solar panels, wiring and other equipment they had accumulated.

"Should we get started building tomorrow?" Nod asked.

"Yeah," Dean replied. "We can probably weld your stand in a day. Cement them in place, then start on ours while we wait for the cement to harden for a few days. Whole thing should be done in a week."

"That will be awesome!" Nod gushed enthusiastically. "Should I ride back with you guys to unload the rest?"

"Nah," Sadie responded. "We'll park the trailer and use the forklift. Easy peazy." Dean nodded in agreement.

They said their goodbyes and left. As they passed the house, Vivian was on the porch waving. Nod walked up carrying his rifle and a small daypack.

"Looks like you got what you were lookin' for," Vivian noticed.

"Yep, right where we thought they would be," Nod acknowledged. "Dean says we could have uninterrupted solar power within a week."

"That's good. We lost power twice today, and it took almost an hour for it to come back up each time."

"Cell phones are out, too. We probably lost the closest tower," Nod surmised.

"Well, it took forever to get service out here to begin with," Vivian replied with exasperation. "Internet must still be working, though. I looked for a recipe a couple minutes ago."

"It's hardwired, so it may last a little longer," Nod mused. "But these frequent blackouts are gonna fry something sensitive eventually. Seems like fewer people are online everyday as the older infrastructure gives out."

"Well, looks like you didn't bring back any stuffed animals for once," Vivian noted.

Nod smiled and reached into his daypack. He pulled out a plush toy Sun wearing sunglasses. "They had them in the solar shop."

CHAPTER 13

Three weeks later

Nod sat on his bed and silently went over the plan one last time. He had the fully charged electric golf cart stashed a half mile north of Vivian's place with the large black duffle bag of supplies inside. From there he would drive to the rig, where he had stashed many months-worth of food. There was a small truck hidden in the tall bushes not far off the road. He would take that to a small teardrop trailer he had hidden a few miles west of that. Then, he would travel north on the many cattle roads and stay up in that area from now on.

It had taken months to get everything in place, but today was the day. He would enjoy the Thanksgiving feast with his friends, excuse himself for a short walk, and be gone forever. They would be sad, but they would get over it.

Nod had made sure Vivian and Lizzy had everything they needed before he left. Their electricity was now fully provided by their solar panels and batteries. Dean and Tex would help with the upkeep, which was minimal. They had solid communications with all the families they worked with via the CB radios. They had enough food in the pantry to last several years. And the firepower Vivian had even before the virus outbreak was impressive.

Nod had questioned his decision to leave many times. It boiled down to two things: he wanted to see the rabbits again, and he didn't think he deserved to be happy with another family. The rabbits, he knew, might not even exist.

He may have imagined them completely, but he really didn't think so. They had always showed up at just the right time and he 'felt' the presence of 'his girls' each time. He wanted that feeling again so badly. He liked Lizzy and Vivian a lot, but they weren't Donna and Dorothy.

Nod stood and straightened the blanket. He scanned the room and found everything in order. He heard Vivian and Lizzy talking in the front room. Thanksgiving festivities took place at the Miller's ranch and both ladies waited on him.

They took Vivian's SUV instead of the Humvee. Vivian didn't like the military vehicle because it wasn't comfortable. Riding in her SUV felt more like taking a short trip.

The Miller's ranch had a large gravel driveway. Nod could see the other groups' Humvees lined up in the driveway as they approached. The Abrams family and Floss family had been invited, too.

The Floss family was headed by Bob, who was seventy years old. None of his children had survived the outbreak, but three of his grandchildren had: Tina and Dina, nineteen year-old twins, and Clint who was twenty-five. In the last two months, they had two different families of survivors move onto their property. Nod didn't know much about them, but he knew there were six more total including an adult man and woman.

The Abrams ranch was furthest south. Cindy was the matriarch and in her 50's. She apparently had to kill her infected husband when he turned. She had two sons, Tom and Abel, who were 25 and 30, respectively, and a daughter, Sophia, who was 24. Abel had a daughter, Glenda, who was 10.

The Abrams group had become the largest when they allowed a large group of survivors to move onto their property. Three adult siblings, Ray, Cindy and Kelly, had escaped Santa Barbara with their four children. Along the way, they had found six more kids of varying ages. Abel and Sophia Abrams, both former Sheriff Deputies, had run into them during a supply run and brought them back to the ranch. They were all living in large trailers on the property.

The Miller's ranch had two layers of fencing and the house had a third layer. Because of this, all the children were playing outside. The Miller's hadn't replaced their dog yet, so Vivian brought Tripod to play with the kids. Nod noticed that even though it was extremely secure, there were four adults outside with rifles watching over them.

When they opened the gate, Lizzy and Tripod ran toward all the kids. Nod and Vivian brought in several armloads of food. A few people met them at the gate and helped lighten their load.

Inside, the mood was jovial and warm. Nod spent time talking to just about everyone. Some he hadn't met yet and got 'their story.' He always managed to change the subject before he was asked about his life prior to the outbreak.

Nod had never eaten so many kinds of foods in his life. Growing up, his family was small, so the gatherings were never big. And you usually just had turkey and stuffing and cranberry sauce. Today he had those staples of Thanksgiving along with tamales, homemade corn tortillas, bratwurst, lamb kabobs, lumpia, and a noodle dish he couldn't pronounce. Someone even managed to find canned pumpkin for pumpkin pie even though the outbreak hit in the summer before pumpkin pie season usually arrived.

Nod sat on the couch with several other men. He had a smile on his face, but inside he felt guilty for enjoying this day. He reassured himself that this would be the last time. One of the older men lamented the fact that there was no football to watch and the others agreed. Then Dean brought a football out of his room and suggested they play their own game. Several people, including Nod, slowly stood up, 'ready' for action.

Yells from outside disturbed Nod's thoughts of gridiron greatness. The front door swung open, revealing Tex half-carrying Millie. Dean rushed over and took hold of his wife. She was in tears, and her shirt was torn. Dean took her to the kitchen where Vivian started to look her over.

"What the hell happened?" Dean yelled to Tex, who was surrounded by the people in the front room.

"We were in the orchard," Tex started, pointing toward the large assortment of trees behind the barn. "Millie wanted to get some more plums. She saw me outside watchin' over the kids and pulled me along. I was picking

126

plums a couple of rows over and thought I heard something. I called to her and she didn't answer, so I ran over there. Someone was attacking her! He had his hand over her mouth and was pulling at her shirt. He saw me with my rifle and dropped her. Ran off toward the west. I got two shots off, but he ran through the trees, so I don't know if I hit anything."

"It was a .... person, not an infected?" Dean asked.

"Yeah. And I'm pretty sure I know who was. He had long stringy red hair and was missin' an ear."

"Shiloh Morton?" several people whispered all at once.

"The Morton's have been gone more than two years," Bob Floss stated. "Are they back?"

"Who are the Morton's?" Nod asked. A few others had the same look on their face.

"The Morton's were the local garbage family around here," Clint Floss explained. "And I mean garbage. Always in trouble, stealin' stuff, hurtin' people."

"There was Max, the dad," Bob Floss remembered. "Tommy, the oldest. Shiloh, who was Dean's age, I believe. And Louisa, the youngest. They all had different mom's because no one could stand to be around Max for very long. Terrible people."

"Except Louisa," Tex added. "She was always nice."

"Yep, she was the black sheep," Bob Floss confirmed. "Well, after the last big fight they started the Sheriff told Max that if he didn't move his family somewhere else, he would charge his boys with assault and see they each did five years."

"Wow, that's some Old West stuff, right there," Nod remarked.

"Yeah, that's how the boss was," Abel Abrams agreed. "And Max wasn't happy, but a week later they were gone. Took all the copper wiring from the house they were renting with them." He put his hand on Tex's shoulder. "Are you sure it was Shiloh?"

"Not 100%, but he did have red hair and he was definitely missing his left ear. Maybe a little skinnier than I remember," Tex said.

"Missing….an ear?" Nod asked.

"He was born without one. Just a hole in the side of his head," Abel remarked.

"Did they live close by?" Nod asked.

"A half mile or so west," Tex stated. "Other side of the orchard. Just a couple of mobile homes."

"Well, we should head over there," Abel Abrams suggested. "Anyone seen Sophia?"

"She's in the kitchen," Nod replied. "I think she's talking to Millie."

"Where's Dean?" Tex asked, looking around.

"Oh, shit!" Nod exclaimed, running to the door. A large group of people followed him.

The virus had affected everyone. Those that didn't die or become murderous monsters had become stronger and faster than normal. The entire group, including the older folks, were running through the orchard like Olympians. Still, Dean was running like a man possessed and they didn't catch up with him until they got to the hovel that used to be the Morton's rented mobile home. Dean was coming out of the hole that used to be a front door.

"No one's here," he spat through gritted teeth. "It's still abandoned."

The assembled group, barely out of breath, began to fan out to search for anyone still in the area. Many had their rifles up to their chests, in the 'ready' position. Nod, who was surprised to find his pistol in his hand, walked up to Dean.

"You're sure there's no one inside?" Nod asked.

"Yeah, it's a small place. Half the walls are gone. Dirt on the floor didn't look disturbed." Dean locked eyes with Nod. "I'm gonna find that son of a bitch and kill 'em."

Nod was conflicted. He had always been against the death penalty. But there weren't jails anymore. How could you protect people you loved? And where did they draw the line? Would they kill thieves, too? At the same time, the way he felt right now, he would probably kill the guy, too.

People began to assemble at the front porch. No one had found anything, but Clint Floss had found some boot prints that were obviously new. Unfortunately, they disappeared onto some dry grass.

"Well, Abel, I know you're not a deputy anymore, but you and Sophia are the closest thing we have," Bob Floss stated. "What should we do about this?"

"Hell guys, I don't really know what we can do," Abel admitted. "We don't have the resources to lock people up."

"I'll kill 'em if I find 'em," Dean warned calmly. A few others nodded in the affirmative.

"I'm not telling you not to," Abel stated. "But remember, we have an eyewitness that's not 100% sure who it was, just a description. Millie might have a better one, but she wasn't around here when the Morton's were around. She doesn't know Shiloh." Abel shook his head. "Like Bob said, I'm not a deputy anymore. I just want you, all of you, to think before you start shootin'. But you can bet your ass if I run into Shiloh Morton anytime soon, well, that's a little too much coincidence for me."

The group broke up and walk back to the Miller's place. Nod saw Bob Floss and his daughter, Tina, standing off to the side, looking at the ground and pointing. He walked over to them and asked them what they were looking at.

"These are the boot prints Clint found," Bob pointed down at the prints, then out over the large, open area covered

130

in dead weeds. "Tina just reminded me that about three miles over there, around the ridge, there's a huge house that used to be owned by the Martino Family Winery. Max worked for them on and off over the years. I think one of his sons came from a dalliance with a cousin to the family or something like that. Anyway, if I was a betting man, I'd be willing to bet that if they were back, they'd be living in that big house."

Millie had recovered by the time Nod returned, even laughing a bit about the whole thing. She confirmed everything Tex had said, adding that the man smelled very strongly of vinegar. Nod and Bob shared a glance but didn't say anything.

Later, as everyone was getting ready to leave, Abel pulled Nod aside. The two went outside to speak. Sophia was already there.

"Listen, Nod, Bob told me about the winery. He said he told you about it. I want to put together a group of people to go over there in the morning."

"Like a posse?" Nod asked.

Abel thought for a moment. "I guess so. Clint Floss and his sister Tina, my brother Tom and I and couple of the guys living with us are going. Sophia is going to hang back and provide fire support, if needed. She's the best distance shooter I know. I want to leave Dean and Tex out of this for now because they're too close to it. Would you like to be part of the 'posse'?"

Nod searched his feelings. What he wanted was to leave here tonight and never look back. Go out into the wilderness and be a hermit or whatever. He had everything in place right now. These people weren't his family. He didn't owe them anything and didn't expect anything from them. They were a means of taking care of Lizzy. Then he thought of Millie, sitting at the kitchen table, and sobbing in her torn clothes.

"What time do we leave?"

CHAPTER 14

The next morning, Nod was already outside when the two Humvees pulled up. He got inside and exchanged 'good mornings' with everyone. There wasn't much talk after that.

Nod was surprised that they drove out to Hwy 46, then turned west. It turned out to be the easiest way to get there as the winery was not far off the highway. The main house was huge and the winery itself was just behind it.

Nod remembered seeing the house on the trip over and back. It had a driveway that was a quarter mile long lined with palm trees. The land around it was now covered in dead or dying grapevines. As they turned onto the driveway, Abel pointed to a small hill roughly half a mile to the east.

"Sophia should already be in place," he stated, picking up the handset for the CB. "Sis, you ready to rock?"

"She's up there?" Nod asked surprised. "She's that good?"

"Yep, good to go," came her reply. "I've seen some movement this morning, but I haven't seen Shiloh. Max is confirmed, as is Tommy. A few others I don't know."

"10-4," Abel replied. "By the way, Nod asked if you could hit anything at that distance."

There was a chuckle over the radio. "Let's hope I don't have to prove it, okay?" came her response.

"Anything else you can tell us?" Abel inquired.

"Yeah, there's two fences around the whole damn house and a pit of some kind in between."

"A moat?" Nod asked with a chuckle.

"Say again?" Abel asked into the handset.

"Two fences with a pit. I know it sounds dumb, but that's what I see."

"Copy that," Abel replied.

Nod scanned the area as the two Humvees approached. The house sprawled but now that they were closer, he could see the fences. The whole area was surrounded by rolling hills with dead grapevines. There were a lot of buildings and equipment behind the main house where most of the winery business got done.

The driveway curved to the front of the house. The first fence, obviously put up in haste, blocked the large front sidewalk steps that went up to the ornate front entrance. The 'pit' Sophia saw was a trench roughly 10 feet deep and five feet wide that appeared to surround the entire house but went under the front steps. Inside the trench were dozens of infected.

"Sis, can you confirm the stairway is the only way into the house?" Abel asked into the handset.

"Roger that," came the reply. "They tore through the sidewalk in back. The only way visible to get to the house is that stairway. I did see a large backhoe behind the house earlier when I was scouting. I'm sure that's how they dug it out."

Three men walked out onto the second-floor balcony. One was older, probably late 50's, with long brown hair that had streaks of gray. Nod figured it was the father, Max. The other two looked similar but were twenty years or so younger and carried rifles. The men began to file out of the two vehicles.

"What you need, boys?" the older man yelled down.

"I'd like to talk to the Martino family," Abel stated.

"And who the hell are you?" the older man asked.

"You know who I am, Max. Deputy Abel Abrams." Abel's frustration was already showing.

"Oh, yeah, I remember you. So, you're the law now?"

"What's left of it, yeah."

"Well, I'm the oldest member of the Martino family left. So, what do you want?" the old man was also visibly annoyed.

"How are you a Martino, exactly?" Abel asked.

"My ex-wife Melissa was a cousin to Stephania Martino, the grandmother to the rest of 'em. They're all dead now, so I took possession of the house and the land. It's all legal-like."

"How do you know they're all dead?" Abel inquired.

"Well, I should say most of them are dead. We found some of the bodies inside. The rest are down in the trench. Not right in their minds, though. But I couldn't bear the thought of puttin' 'em down, so I stashed them in the trench so they could still be close to the rest of the family." Max pretended to wipe a tear from his eye.

"I see. Well, I need to speak with your boy, Shiloh."

"Funny you should mention him, Mr. Deputy. Somebody shot him yesterday when he was out for a walk. Put a hole in his thigh. He's gonna pull through, but I'm glad you happened by, so I didn't have to search for someone to report it to. There's dangerous people about. That's why we have the fences."

Abel grew more frustrated. "I need to speak with him about that. Can you bring him out?"

"He can't walk very well. I'd invite you up, but we seem to have misplaced the key to the gates. I think Shiloh had them when he limped in yesterday. When I find the keys, I'll come find you." Max had a fake sad grin on his face.

"We can take care of that lock for you," Abel stated, walking over to the Humvee, and pulling a pair of bolt cutters out of the back.

Suddenly armed people started pouring out of the doors behind Max. They lined the balcony, pointing their rifles down at the two vehicles. Max chuckled.

"Your family has grown," Abel sneered through clenched teeth.

"I made some friends after we moved. On the way here, we came across a caravan of troop carriers outside of Vandenberg. They were all dead but there were lots of weapons. Some bigger than others."

When he finished his last sentence, there was a loud 'whump' and something streaked across the sky. It impacted half a mile away from them in the middle of the vineyard and exploded, shooting wood and dirt far into the air. The men all jumped, pulling their rifles up. Abel put his hands out to calm them.

"Those bastards have mortars!" someone yelled from behind Nod.

"I think it's time you fellas took off. Before someone 'accidentally' gets hurt." Max's sad grin was replaced with a broader, more deviant sneer.

"This ain't over, Max!" Abel shouted.

"For your sake, Mr. Deputy, it better be," he replied.

***

"So, we're not gonna do anything?" Dean asked.

Judging from the murmurs alone, those assembled in the Miller's living room were as incredulous as Dean. They had gathered there after returning from the winery. Dean, Tex, Sadie and Millie were also in attendance now.

"I didn't say we would do nothing, just that our choices are limited," Abel explained.

"Screw this! I'm gonna go over there and pull that red-headed bastard out of the house myself!" Dean warned.

"You in a hurry to make Millie a widow?" Sophia asked. "There were 10 armed men on that balcony plus at least two more behind the house operating the mortar. Plus Max. Plus any others that were still inside. At least thirteen armed men with automatic weapons, sniper rifles and mortar shells."

"Plus, we don't know what other goodies they stole from the caravan," Abel continued. "They may have night vision or rocket-propelled grenades. Hell, they could have drones for all we know."

Clint Floss chimed in, "Some mortars can do damage up to four miles away. We don't know what type they have, but we may be in their firing range right now."

Nod was alarmed. He knew Vivian's house was over five miles from the winery. But if they could hit a target from over three miles away, they could hit any one of their places without being anywhere nearby.

"You'd need a really good mortar guy to hit anything accurately at that distance. I doubt they're that good," Sophia suggested. "What worries me most is I saw at least one APC parked in a barn behind the house. Those have serious armor. We don't have anything that can pierce one of those babies, let alone stop it."

"So, we need better firepower?" Dean asked. "There's a few military bases around here we could raid."

"According to the people we took in, Vandenberg is overrun with infected," Abel said. "And anything else around here is just National Guard bases. Mostly just guns and Humvees. That's where most of our hardware came from. They don't even keep live grenades on those bases most of the time, other than smokers."

Nod had grenades. Six of them, but he wasn't going to volunteer that knowledge to anyone. He was formulating a plan, but he wanted to see how this discussion went.

"Listen, Shiloh has to pay for what he did to Millie and what he was gonna do to her," Dean stated. "We have to do something."

A young man Nod didn't know half-raised his hand to interrupt. "My Name's Ray Testor. I haven't had a chance to speak with everyone to introduce myself yet." The young man's shaky voice showed his uneasiness at speaking to the group.

"It's alright, Ray," Abel assured him. "What's up?"

"Well," the young man started. "I'm pretty sure we ran into this guy, Max, on the road. He's really bad news."

"What happened?" Sophia asked.

"Some of you already know, but me, my brother Kelly, my sister Cindy and our kids, came up here from

Valencia. We walked most of the way to Vandenberg because we heard there was a relief camp there. When we got there, it was overrun with infected inside the fence. Probably thousands, maybe tens of thousands. There was a long caravan of military vehicles that was stopped at the gate like they wouldn't let them inside. It looked like there'd been a big fight there. Bullet casings and soldier bodies all over the place. Everyone in the trucks was dead."

"That sounds terrible," Sadie said, shaking her head in disbelief.

"We were hiding in a building there, eating some lunch when we heard a truck coming up the road. It was this Max character and the people with him. They were in two big trucks and parked next to the Humvees. The started going through the vehicles, looking for stuff. They pulled out all kinds of things. I couldn't see exactly what they had but some of it was rifles. They were loading their trucks up when someone got a big armored vehicle started. Then they started transferring boxes and bags to it."

"The APC you saw," Abel nodded to Sophia who nodded back.

"Max saw something he wanted just inside the fence. He was telling a young girl, probably early teens, something, and it was pretty heated because the girl kept shaking her head no. Max smacked her real hard and dragged her over to the fence. The other guys started getting the infected attention a few hundred feet down the fence. When they

140

moved away, she climbed over the fence. It was tall but didn't have any razor wire or anything."

"What was she going for?" Dean asked.

"I don't know for sure. The boxes had writing on them, but we couldn't read it. They must have been heavy, though, because she picked one up and started to walk slowly with it back to the fence. She tried to climb up but dropped the box. The infected heard it hit and ran over when they saw the girl. She screamed as they tore her apart."

There was a gasp in the room as realization set in for some. "Was the girl blonde, about 5 feet tall?" Tex asked.

"Sounds about right," Ray replied. "The man just stood there and watched. Didn't fire a shot to slow the infected. Didn't even put the poor girl out of her misery. He just walked away as soon as she stopped screaming. He started barking orders to the other guys like nothing happened. They left not long after."

Tex lowered his head. "That was Louise," he said weakly. "He was always making her do stupid stuff like that." Sadie rubbed his shoulders.

"He let his own daughter die?" Millie asked incredulously.

"That Max has always been a real SOB," Abel said, glancing over at Sophia with a raised eyebrow. "Still, as much as it kills me to say it, we're just going to have to wait and watch for now. We'll keep an eye on them and when the timing is right, we'll react. Until then, we need to watch out for each other."

"I can't believe this!" Dean exploded.

"Look at me, Dean," Sophia demanded, standing eye to eye with him. "Tell me you're not going to do something. Right here." She pointed to her eyes. "Look right here and tell me, on your honor, that you are not going to do something that might put this house in the firing line."

Dean was crest fallen. He looked at Millie, whose eyes were pleading with him to agree, and then at Sadie and Tex. "I'll agree that I'm not going to attack that house, but I can't guarantee that if I see Shiloh anywhere outside their fence, I won't shoot him dead."

"Good enough for now," Abel agreed with a nod.

A few minutes later, the assembly began to break up. Abel checked with Dean again before he left to be sure he still intended to comply. Being satisfied with his answer, he and Sophia and the rest of their group headed off toward the door.

A few seconds later, Sophia returned saying she forgot her jacket. Pulling it off the back of the chair she had been sitting in, she paused and turned to Dean.

"I'm on record that responding right now is reckless, but if you two decide you have to do something, count me in. I couldn't sleep at night if I didn't help."

142

"Thanks, Sophia," Dean replied with a sad smile.

She stared at he and Nod for a half-second, then walked out. A few minutes later, Dean, Nod, and Tex followed. They sat quietly on the front porch while inside the ladies straightened up the house as Vivian and Lizzy got ready to go to. Nod looked over at Dean.

"You're not going to let it go, are you?" Nod asked.

"Could you?" Dean replied, then turned to look at Nod. "I mean, you've never talked about it before, but I've always had the feeling you used to be married."

"Used to be a very different person," Nod stated without confirming Dean's suspicions. "I never touched a gun, never believed in violence as a solution for anything. I was content to go through life letting my parents, then my wife, the government, Hell, anyone else, take care of everything. Well, almost everything." His eyes welled up thinking of Donna and Dorothy. "But it's a different world. A more dangerous place. That family, the Morton's, their existence makes it a more dangerous place. For Lizzy and Vivian. For you guys. If you want to go after them, I'm with you. I just have one requirement."

"What's that?"

"When you're ready to do it, it's just you and me. No one else." He looked over at Tex.

"Screw that!" Tex yelled, then lowered his voice. "I won't let my brother do this without me."

"Tex, if we fail, if any of them survive, where do you think they're coming first for payback?" Nod stared at him with a serious look. "There's a good chance we won't be coming back. Your mom and Millie are tough and smart, but they still need you. There's no reason for your mom to lose both her sons."

"I agree," Dean affirmed. "Tex, it's a big responsibility we're puttin' on you, I know. But if things go south, you'll have to get mom and Millie to the Abrams farm. That's the safest place. Can you do that for me, bro?"

Tex had tears in his eyes. "I can do that, bro. You can count on me." Dean gave his brother a side hug as Tex wiped his eyes with the back of his hands. "So, when should we do this?"

"Day after tomorrow," Nod stated. "No reason to put it off. I'm busy in the morning but I'll come by tomorrow afternoon and we can talk about what we're gonna do."

CHAPTER 15

Nod went to the Miller farm late in the afternoon. It was much later than he had expected to, but he had spent that morning running a lot of errands in anticipation of their assault. Still, he offered no explanation but simply stated he was sorry he was so late.

The plan they came up with was simple. They would attack in the low light of dawn, moving in from opposite sides of the house and using Sophia to spot trouble through her sniper scope. Molotov cocktails would be tossed into the house repeatedly and people would be picked off as they exited. The rest would die in the blaze.

Dean had spent the afternoon gathering everything they needed for the Molotovs and had contacted Sophia in person to make sure she was still in. Nod would pick Dean up at 5AM and they would be in place by 5:30. Sophia would make her own way to her perch up on the hill.

After their meeting and dinner, Nod sat on the porch with Sadie. They were quiet, enjoying the cool night air and sipping a couple of bottles of beer. Nod could tell Sadie wanted to say something but was hesitating. Finally, she broke the silence.

"You know, Nod, we really don't know anything about you. Your life before the virus, I mean."

"I'm a man of mystery, alright," Nod replied with a smile. "It's part of my charm."

"Come on, I know it's not easy, but it would be nice to know a little more about you. You seem like such a helpful guy. I bet you were a teacher."

Nod laughed. . "No, I wasn't a teacher!" The smile stayed on his face as he remembered his former life. "I will tell you the man I used to be was a writer of sorts. Mostly online tech articles."

"What was your name?" she asked with some exasperation.

"Depends on who you ask. But 'Nod' was the one I answered to the most, so that's who I chose to be now."

"Why are helping us? I mean, there's a good chance you'll die tomorrow, and you jumped at it." Sadie had tears in her eyes. Nod knew those tears were for Dean, not him. Well, maybe him a little, too.

"To tell you the truth, Sadie, I'm only alive because I promised two very special people that I wouldn't kill myself." Nod's eyes had their own tears now. "You guys are the closest thing I have to a family, so risking my life is a no-brainer. I don't have a death wish. If we win tomorrow, my new family survives another day. If we lose, well, I should have been dead six months ago. No big loss, really. I will guarantee you one thing, though."

"What's that?"

"Your boy won't die tomorrow."

146

"You can't guarantee that, Nod," she declared, looking away from him.

Nod stood up and started down the stairs. "Believe me, Sadie, one way or another, Dean will make it home." Nod stopped and thought for a moment. "Ya know, I think, maybe, the only reason I'm still alive is be there tomorrow. Weird." He opened the door to his Humvee. "Tell Dean I'll be here at five. See you then."

Sadie waved with a forced smile. She had an idea of what Nod meant, but she wasn't sure and decided not to tell Dean what he had said.

***

Nod slept even though, it could be his last day on Earth. He rose early and had loaded the Humvee and returned for one more trip when Vivian met him on the porch.

"Well, I guess you're going to get your wish," she stated enthusiastically.

"What's that?" Nod replied.

"To die, of course," Vivian said, now stone-faced.

Nod was thrown. "We have a shot. We might just make it."

"You're not planning to make it, Nod. You and I both know it. You packed up everything in your room and even made the bed. In all the months you've lived here you've never been so neat. And you've been all smiles since you got

147

home last night. You clung to Lizzy until she fell asleep and I heard you giving her a long goodbye just now. She's still asleep."

Well, I'm just plannin' for the worst," Nod defended himself.

"You can't bullshit someone who's spent most of their life up to their elbows in the real thing, Nod. I know you were planning to leave at some point. I saw the duffle bag in the closet. But it's still there. What are you planning, kiddo?"

Nod thought for a minute. Vivian was no fool and could always tell when he was hiding something. "Alright, cards on the table, Doc."

Nod spent a few minutes outlining his plan for the assault. He went into detail. Vivian's attention was rapt on his words. Her face didn't betray her feelings one way or another. When he finished, he paused to let her reply.

"Sounds like you've thought of everything," she stated simply. "Except how you'll survive."

Nod was surprised again. "I thought you would try and talk me out of it."

"Could I?" Vivian gave him a raised eyebrow. "Just tell me one thing, and I'll walk back into the house and not bother you again."

"Shoot."

"What was her name? The one you lost."

He hadn't spoken their names out loud since they died. "There were two. Donna and Dorothy, my wife and daughter." His voice broke as he said it.

"And would they want you to die?"

"That's two things, Vivian," Nod intoned, picking up his last box.

Vivian stood on the step above him, grabbed his head, and hugged it to her chest. "You damn, stupid man!" she stage-whispered, and kissed the top of his head. Then she let him go.

"I'll miss you, too, Doc," Nod professed. "Hug Lizzy for me." He drove away with Vivian still standing on the porch.

***

"You missed the turn," Dean pointed out.

"Oh shit, I forgot to tell you! I have some grenades!" Nod burst out loud.

"No way!"

"I found them in a duffle bag a few weeks after the virus hit. Stashed them in the rig I was sleeping in at the time and forgot them when I left. There's six of them."

"That's awesome! Do we have time to pick them up? Is it close?"

"Just a few miles away from here. Shouldn't take but a few minutes."

The few miles to Al's rig took ten minutes. Nod had returned to the rig several times since originally leaving including yesterday. He pulled up to the rig and pointed to the passenger door.

"They're sitting in a duffle bag in the passenger seat. Could you grab 'em real quick?" Nod asked.

"Sure," Dean replied, hopping out of the Humvee and climbing up to open the rig's door. Inside was very dark and Dean felt around the seat for the bag. Instead, he found a sheet of paper. When he raised it up to look at it, Nod suddenly sped off, kicking up dirt and rocks as the tires spun.

"What the—?" Dean's question died in his throat. He jumped down and ran after Nod, but the Humvee was too fast. He stared off at the Humvee until the taillights were no longer visible. Then he shook his head and headed back to the rig.

The paper was sitting on the ground under the door. He picked it up and could see writing on it. He pulled out a small flashlight to read it.

"Dear Dean, sorry but I couldn't let you do this. I have the grenades and a few other toys. I have a plan of attack that has a good chance of success and it doesn't require you putting yourself in harm's way. There is a rifle in the driver's seat of the rig and if you walk four miles west, you will find the Humvee. I'm switching cars there and I'll leave

150

the keys in it. If I don't make it, please help Vivian with Lizzy. I know you will be a good dad. Thanks, Nod."

"No, no, no, NO!" Dean danced angrily. He grabbed the rifle from the rig and began running toward the waiting Humvee.

***

The car that Nod stashed the day before was an electric golf cart. A very 'fancy' electric golf cart they had found months ago along with half a dozen others just like it. There was a company nearby that made custom golf carts, some electric, some gas-powered, and this one was one of their nicest with larger tires, four-wheel drive, stronger batteries for greater speed and distance and room for four. Most importantly for Nod's purposes tonight, it was completely silent. After he taped up the lights, it was a perfect stealthy machine.

It took him only a few minutes to get to the Morton house. He sat in the golf cart at the end of the driveway and scanned the house. It was still too dark to see much, but there was some flickering light inside that indicated they were using candles, which was exactly what Nod had hoped.

He had spent some time researching night-vision rifle scopes and found that even the best scopes only allowed the hunter to see three hundred yards or so. That assumed there was no UV lamp in the distance to help and according to Nod's own cheap night vision monocle, there were no UV lamps anywhere around the house. The end of the driveway was well outside their view at night.

On the ground in front of him were a fleet of drones he had picked up yesterday morning. They were set up in waves, with each group having a part to play in the attack. Nod hit the microphone button on his shoulder.

"Are you in position, Red Leader?" he asked.

"Red Leader?" Sophia's voice laughed softly in his ear. "Ah, a fellow Star Wars fan. Then you're Gold Leader?"

"Why not? And Blue Leader has been safely stashed at the rig. Are you ready?"

"I bet he wasn't happy."

"I didn't wait around and see."

"Well, I'm dialed in. Ready on your mark."

"Sending in the first wave now." Nod had visited Sophia and told him his plan after his trip to the hobby shop. She had agreed to help him since his plan was better than Dean's and required only Nod to be placed in danger.

Nod hummed Handel's "Flight of the Valkyrie" as the sudden rise and run of the first four quadcopter drones reminded him of a scene from *Apocalypse Now*. Each drone carried nearly a gallon of diesel fuel in old milk jugs attached by strings. They struggled to get airborne at first, but eventually sailed up and off toward the house.

Since the lights had all been taped up, Nod had to follow the drones by the high pitch of their engines. They were programmed to hover at 60 feet, and he moved them over the top of the house as best he could. The cameras on the bottom sent a live feed to his tablet, but it wasn't a great picture in the dark. The light coming from the windows was barely visible from above.

He did his best to position two drones over the front balcony and two over the back balcony, then he cut their engines off. They fell like rocks and smashed on the hard tiles, spilling diesel everywhere. The back balcony erupted in flames as the wrecked drones ignited the diesel. Diesel burns slowly and is hard to put out, so Nod knew it would be good to start the house on fire, but also give them some light.

Unfortunately, the front balcony didn't ignite. He knew it was possible since it required a spark and the mostly plastic drones didn't usually throw off sparks when they crashed. They had gotten lucky with the back balcony.

"Alright Red Leader send one to the front," Nod ordered into the mic. He tossed the tablet and picked up another one. Four more drones rose into the air and headed toward the house.

From somewhere on the dark hill half a mile east, a single, red line shot over to the balcony with a thud. After a full second, the front balcony ignited.

"Gotta watch where those tracers land. They might start a fire," Nod stated sarcastically into the mic.

"Especially a .50 caliber tracer," Sophia added. "How's your view of the APC?"

"Perfect. The back balcony is lit up like a lamp. I'm sending it a care package now."

One of the drones in the air peeled off and headed straight for the APC parked in the back. Hanging from the bottom was a string attached to the pin on a grenade. The pin had been bent so that it would take less force to remove it. The drone hit just under the front of the APC and tumbled, pulling the pin from the grenade. A few seconds later, the front of the APC lifted off the ground with the explosion.

"APC disabled, Gold Leader," Sophia stated. "Be warned, you have two people exiting the front with rifles. Three or four on each balcony trying to put the fire out. And three just exited the back, looking at the APC. What do you want to?"

"Death from above, Red Leader." With that, Nod cut the engines to the other three drones. One fell near the APC and one on each balcony. Nod tossed the tablet and started driving toward the house. "Let me know what happens."

A few seconds later, each grenade detonated. "I think you killed all three by the APC. None are moving. Back balcony collapsed. No movement there, either. Front balcony has a hole in it, but it didn't fall. No movement."

"OK," Nod responded. "After the crash, you take out anything still moving, unless it's me."

"Roger that," Sophia replied.

Nod sped down the drive. He glanced over at the propane bottles that filled the other three seats and grabbed four road flares. He lit each one and tossed them in the seats.

The driveway ended, and the stairway came into view. The golf cart crashed through the first gate, then the second. Nod managed to keep it on the sidewalk despite the constant bouncing and shifting of the bottles. One of the flares hit his right thigh and burned a hole in his pants.

"Owww!" Nod shouted, taking a hand off the wheel to move the flare. He looked back just as the front doors came into view. He rolled out of the seat and onto the sidewalk a second before the golf cart smashed through the entry.

Nod landed hard and rolled. He slowly rose and pulled his pistol. He raised it and advanced toward the smashed doorway.

"Behind you!" Sophia shouted. Nod spun when he was hit by a Crazy. The impact knocked the gun from his hand and the two sprawled on the ground. Another Crazy approached when its chest suddenly exploded outward in a glowing mess and it collapsed.

"I can take out the ones climbing up but not the one on top of you. Too close!" Sophia screamed in his ear.

Nod pushed the Crazy off, and it skidded away. He glanced at the trench and saw one of the gates had fallen into it. Crazies were feverishly trying to climb up, but most were not coordinated enough to do it. The Crazy came back at

155

Nod, who delivered a swift front kick to its midsection. It fell back a few steps, and Nod scanned the ground for his pistol, but the light from the fire was fading.

Someone grabbed Nod from behind and pulled him into the house through the door. He was thrown backward on the hard tile floor. It was Max and he quickly spun around and shot the Crazy in the head.

"You made me kill my cousin, Ezra," he stated with measured voice. "Well, my ex-wife's second cousin, Ezra. Always hated the prick but I loved watching him run around in the pit." He stared at Nod in the low light. "I don't know you, but you were with the deputy. You a Dodger fan?" He pointed at Al's ever-present hat on Nod's head.

"Not really a baseball fan," Nod replied.

Sophia's voice rang into Nod's ear. "Nod, the rest are trapped in the trench still! I can't see you! Are you by the cart? I can't see passed the cart!"

"Always hated the Dodgers," Max stated, raising the gun to point at Nod's head.

"Just one second?" Nod asked, raising an index finger.

"Gonna' plead for your life, Dodger fan?"

Nod strained and reached as if to rub his shoulder. Instead, he keyed the mic. "Nope, gonna end yours," he stated with no waver in his voice. "Send two to the cart."

Max squinted his eyes trying to understand what Nod meant. Half a second later, one shot hit the cart followed quickly by another. There was little time to even react. Nod wasn't sure what ignited the propane tanks. The tracer rounds or the smoldering flares, but faster than Max could flinch, a fireball erupted outward from the cart. Nod closed his eyes waiting for the inevitable. Three concussive blasts threw him around like a rag doll. Then there was no sound at all.

***

Nod stood by the rig. Dumbfounded, he looked around and saw the two rabbits hopping around the scrub. He ran to them and followed until they disappeared into the brush. His dropped his head and saw he was by his girl's graves.

"Nod?" came a soft familiar voice behind him.

He turned to see Donna and Dorothy standing there. Surprisingly, he shed no tears. He was happy and ran the few feet to them. They all three embraced.

"I've missed you two. My girls," Nod stated.

"We've been with you the whole time, daddy," Dorothy replied. "Right here." She pointed to his heart.

"I felt you, pumpkin. Both of you." He hugged them both tightly. "I feel so weird. I should be blubbering, but I feel very calm."

"No tears in this place, honey," Donna explained. "But I'm afraid you're not staying. It's not your time."

"But I want to stay. I'm happy here," Nod pleaded.

"You can be happy there, too, Nod. You just have to let yourself. The best thing you can do for us is to live. And live well." Donna's voice was so warm to his ears.

"Yeah, daddy. Lizzy seems great! And Vivian would have been an awesome grandma!" Dorothy exclaimed.

"You have a family there, Nod. They didn't replace us, our family just got bigger," Donna stated.

"Will I see you again? The rabbits?" Nod asked.

"You never know, my love. You never know." Donna's words faded with the world around him.

***

Nod woke to someone pushing hard on his chest. He coughed and sputtered. He opened his eyes and, slowly, Deans sweaty face came into view. Tears streamed down his cheeks.

"You son of a bitch! I can't believe you did this!" Dean yelled at him.

"Did we win?" Nod asked weakly.

"I'd say we did," Dean replied, scanning the area.

Nod sat up with Dean's help and looked around. It was brighter now as the sun peaked up over the hills. He was covered in bricks and dirt. Behind him, most of the huge house was no longer standing.

CHAPTER 16

Dean and Sophia took Nod back to Vivian's farm. He was in and out of consciousness for hours as she worked on him. When he could finally keep his eyes open more than a few minutes, it was already getting dark outside.

"Well, look who's comin' around," Sadie noticed. She sat next to him in a chair, a book on her lap.

"Sadie? How long have I…?" Nod's voice trailed off.

"You've been out most of the day. Half of our community has been by here so far. Sophia had a hell of story to tell about you two. I mean, drones? Shit, that's wild."

"How long have you been waiting?" Nod asked.

"Don't get any funny ideas, champ." She winked at him. "I'm just takin' my turn at your bedside so Vivian could rest up." She turned her head to the door. "Tex, call Vivian!"

Tex yelled an affirmative from outside the door. It was then that he realized he was in the barn, where Vivian's makeshift surgery room was.

"How bad am I?"

"You've been better. She had to do surgery on your left arm. It had a bone sticking out of it, but it turned out it wasn't yours. Yours was broken very badly, though. Your left hip was dislocated, but it's back where it's supposed to be. Half your hair was burned off. So, I shaved the rest while you were asleep. Vivian thinks our supped-up recuperative abilities will help you. You'll probably be fine in a few weeks."

Vivian came in and asked for some privacy so she could examine Nod. They spoke as she worked, and her prognosis lined up with what Sadie had said. She also let it slip that Sadie had been sitting by his side for most of the day.

***

Three days later, Nod sat in a recliner in Vivian's living room while nearly everyone in their community visited. Some were sitting in the same room, while others were in the kitchen or on the porch.

"Don't make me laugh!" Nod pleaded. "It hurts my ribs."

"I'm not kidding, Nod. You left a smoke trail in the air as you flew through the door!" Sophia recounted. "Ask Dean, he saw it."

"It's true," Dean confirmed from his seat on the couch next to Tex. "He skidded to a halt right in front of me, head still smokin'."

"And you brought me back to life," Nod said, smiling.

Dean blushed. "Shoot, I was just punching you in the chest for leaving me behind."

"Then why the mouth-to-mouth?" Sophia asked.

"And why did you use so much tongue?" Nod added. Another round of laughs rang out as Dean blushed harder.

After the laughter died down, Abel started, "I've been meaning to ask you, Nod, could you tell if it was the flares or the tracer rounds that ignited the tanks? I've seen people try and blow up propane tanks by shooting them and they usually just blow a hole in them."

"It happened too fast, to tell you the truth. I heard the rounds strike the tanks, but the explosions happened too fast to tell."

"I'm surprised you remember anything," Sadie remarked. "How do you feel?"

"My hip doesn't hurt at all anymore. My back still aches a bit, and my arm is still pretty bad." He pointed to the thick padding surrounding his left arm.

"The scars on your head are fading, too," Millie pointed out.

"Good to know we can recover so quickly. I mean, I assume we all would," Sophia noted.

"Vivian says we should all heal similarly," Sadie said.

"Too bad all those drones were destroyed. I'd love to get my hands on some of those babies," Tex lamented.

"Plenty more at the hobby shop," Nod added. "We'll go as soon as my arm is better."

"Definitely!" Tex exclaimed.

"By the way, Nod, we got you something," Abel said, reaching for a brown paper bag. "Your hat got burned to a crisp and it's weird seeing you without it. So, we got you this." He tossed the bag onto Nod's lap.

Nod was surprised by the gesture. He opened the bag and found a brand-new blue ball cap except this one had the Dodgers logo on it. "Thanks guys, you don't know what this means to me." His eyes began to tear up and he wiped then on his sleeve.

"You must have been a heck of a fan," Dean observed, wiping his own watery eyes.

"Not really," Nod replied, placing the hat on his head, and wincing a bit from the not-quite-healed burns. "In fact, I don't think I ever saw them play."

"Then why do you wear that hat all the time?" Sadie asked.

Nod thought for a moment. "Well, it all started with a trip to the beach......"

Nod and Co. will return in

"The Land of Nod 2: And the Sea Gave Up the Dead"

About the Author

Robert M Whitbey grew up in Shafter, CA. He attended California State University, Bakersfield, the University of Wyoming and Point Loma University. He has been a high school science teacher for over a decade and an adjunct college professor for half that time. Prior to that he spent many years working in agricultural research. His hobbies include reading, writing, gardening and golf.

Rob has published several books in the past few years. His first, *How to Become a Reluctant Prepper and Why it's OK to be One*, was published under his pen name, The Reluctant Prepper. His second book and first novel, *The Angel,* is a superhero fantasy novel based in California's Central Valley. *The Vessel* continues the Small Town Heroes series on Laramie, WY. The third novel in the series, *The Soldier*, took place in Redmond, OR.

Rob's latest novel, before this one, is called *The Competition*. It is actually two stories told in parallel. The first involves a high school teacher that must get his students home on foot from far away after a catastrophe. The second involves the teacher's wife dealing with the catastrophe in their community. Near the end, the two stories merge.

His favorite modern authors are Peter Clines, DJ Molle and Dennis E Taylor.

Rob currently resides in Bakersfield, CA with his wife, Lacy, and their two sons, Dylan and Jack.

Please visit the authors' Facebook page for more info or to contact the author. Questions and comments are always welcome.